THE DAY THE GODS WEPT

by

Eugenia Collier

Eugenia Collier
2022

THE DAY THE GODS WEPT

ISBN-13: 9781542657518

ISBN-10: 1542657512

Cover Design: jackholdenbooks.com

TDTGW4

EUGENIA COLLIER

ACKNOWLEDGMENTS

This work has worn many faces. It started as an
emotional jolt, a deeply human response to coming
face to face with tragedy, even ancient tragedy. I was
a tourist among many other tourists, visiting the ruins
of the Roman town Pompeii, which was destroyed
more than 2,000 years ago by a volcanic eruption but
centuries later was excavated and was now a tourist
attraction. We explored the people's homes, their
religion, their history, and their most intimate lives.
Most wrenching were the plaster casts of people in
their final agony, as the burning lava flowed over
them and later hardened, recording for each, the
moment of death. Centuries later, long after the flesh
had rotted away, the hardened lava remained.
Giuseppe Fiorelli, the leader of the excavation project
which had resulted from the discovery of the lost city,
ordered that plaster of Paris be pumped into the
cavities left by the rotted-away flesh, providing
perfect molds of each individual, casts to be viewed
by generations unborn as another clue to the mystery
of death. I--a tourist--was particularly moved by the
cast of a young girl in a short dress, her knees drawn
up as in a fetal position, her hands clasped over her
mouth in a primordial scream, her eyes wide, staring
at approaching flaming doom. What was this girl's

life like until this unimaginable moment? What were her dilemmas, her hopes, her pain?

Many months later, researching into the ancient world which had suddenly beckoned me, I discovered that this plaster of Paris cast was not that of a young girl in a short dress but of a man in a tunic. Well, what difference did that make? By then my emotion had gelled into a sketch that I felt compelled to write. My central character Valeria-Julia (the "girl" in the short dress) had taken shape, had a past and a present, and was as real to me as any young person, then or now. The writing was underway. As it progressed, the work developed from a sketch to a short story to a long story to a novella to a short novel. I hope that by now it has finished growing.

A number of friends and advisors have contributed to this work's existence. I am grateful to each one individually and to all collectively for their friendship, their faith in me, and their constant encouragement. I am particularly grateful to these:

Emmett Chappelle, long-time friend and fellow tourist to Pompeii, whose encouragement and practical suggestions kept me moving every step of the way;

Natalie Stokes-Peters, who helped me to understand some of the mysteries of publication and who even believed that I was really going to complete this work;

Jacqueline McLenden-Brooks, who edited the first version of this work and helped me to realize that I still had a lot of work to do;

Cecelia Fedd, who gave me valuable help with some of the time-consuming and energy-sapping drudgery involved in doing research; and to Coppin State University in Baltimore for granting her an internship to help me with this project in her senior year;

Judith Willner, who suggested my work as Cecelia's internship and was consistently encouraging and vitally interested in my progress;

The Charlestown Writers Critique Group----Denis and Diana Holden, Jodi and Geno Primoff, Maxine Guertler, Steve Schimpff, Karl Lamb, Millie Kreider, Charles Wright, and Mat Merker---for their close attention to the manuscript, for their perceptive suggestions, and for their encouragement. I am especially grateful to Denis Holden for facilitating the publication of this novel. Without him this work would still be a yellowing manuscript in a cluttered file drawer.

DEDICATED

TO

Emmett W. Chappelle
with love

PROLOGUE

What hiding-place do we look to, what help, if the earth itself is causing the ruin, if what protects us, upholds us, on which cities are built, which some speak of as a kind of foundation of the universe, separates and reels?

Seneca, ancient Roman philosopher

The old folk say: Before people walked the world, Sky and Earth mated, and they gave birth to a race of giants. Oh, they were fearful, those giants! They grew and grew. They became stronger and stronger until they thought that the only thing that mattered was who could be the strongest. For their mother was the eternal earth, and their father was the endless sky. But of the children of Earth and Sky, who would be mightiest? After a while they began to argue, then to fight about who should have dominion over the others. So they fought, but none could subdue the others. Finally they decided that instead of fighting each other, they should join forces, and among them, they could conquer the universe.

By now they had grown mad with their lust for power. In their madness, they lost their sense. For only the gods were more powerful than the giants. So the giants got together and in their arrogance, they challenged the gods. But the gods were just as arrogant and just as certain that the only thing that counted was power.

The conflict between the giants and the gods shook the world and split the sky. First one side and then the other would prevail. Eventually the gods won. They always do, The gods returned the defeated giants to their mother Earth, imprisoning them in the depths of the mighty mountain Vesuvius.

But the giants would not be silenced forever. They became restless, even at the bottom of the mountain with all that earth above them. They writhed against their imprisonment. They moved around. When they moved, the earth trembled. And now and then, every few centuries, the giants' rage broke through the tons of earth. And Vesuvius vomited earth's detritus, and it poured down the mountainside, destroying all living things.

EUGENIA COLLIER

I

THE DAY THE GODS WEPT

She had always loved the mountain. It loomed
above them, ever-present, so that wherever you went
in the city, the mountain was always there, awesome
in its majestic beauty. It protected them and nurtured
them, its bulk providing a barrier from harsh winds,
its fecund fields covered with grape arbors and rich
vegetation. Cattle roamed freely and multiplied. The
mountain teemed with life and fertility and joy. The
mountain, the sparkling bay that rimmed the city, the
soft breezes that caressed her hair--they were the only
certainty she knew.

For she was not even certain of her name. Valeria-
Julia. Which twin was she, Valeria or Julia? No one
had been able to tell the babies apart except the
mother, whose stiffened arms the people had had to
break in order to separate the barely-alive from the
newly-dead. Sometimes even now, in nightmares she
felt the icy clasp. She felt the earth tremble and heard
the crash of her world shattered and saw her reality
turn red. She heard the cries and then listened to the
roaring silence.

She had been a toddler, found by neighbors in the
ruins among the scattered dead. Which twin was she,
Valeria or Julia? Which had died and which had

lived? She had responded to both names. Was she--somehow--both? The people called her Valeria-Julia. There was a duality about her as if two people inhabited one body. She was ever aware of the Other, tugging her in one direction when she wanted to go in another. "Valeria-Julia can't make up her mind," often grumbled Marcella, who had taken the hurt, homeless child when nobody else would. Yet as she grew older she was increasingly aware of a sense of incompleteness, as if some vital part of her were missing--or hidden--and she had to keep searching for something unknown.

But when she sat gazing at the mountain she felt a profound sense of peace and joy. The restlessness was quieted; both halves of herself, for the moment, were merged and were reconciled.

On this stifling August night, Valeria-Julia had slept fitfully. Wisps of the old nightmare had pierced her slumber, and she awoke struggling upright, gasping and sweating, caught between realities. A throbbing pain pulsed inside her head, the familiar staring into the blackness until sleep conquered her again, sucked her back to the day when the earth shook, when Valeria and Julia had merged and, never knowing which twin she was, she became both.

By morning she was exhausted. Her throat was raw as if she had been screaming for hours as she had on the night they had found her in the rubble seventeen years ago, a baby clinging to a dead baby, the blood of the living and the blood of the dead intermingled, open- mouthed and mute because no more screams could come.

Now she crawled heavily off the mattress which she and Marcella shared. She struggled to her feet. Her swollen eyes were only half open. Her mouth tasted foul. She stumbled to the fragment of mirror on the table across the room. In the near darkness of early morning, her image in the mirror was dim and distorted like the remnants of old fear. Her hair hung limply over her eyes, black pools in her pale face. The scar was hidden, but she was, as usual, aware of it-- the still-livid scar in the middle of her forehead, from her hairline curling at the bottom to her left brow. Ugly, ugly. The visible reminder of the day of the earthquake when her life, like her forehead, had been split in two.

Behind her, she heard old Marcella's snore, sonorous and rhythmic like the break of waves on sand. The snore was strangely comforting. It had always been there, to the farthest reaches of Valeria-Julia's memory. For it had been Marcella, already half-blind and, they said, half-crazy, who had taken in the double-named orphan, washed her and bandaged her, and held her to the sagging bosom that first night and many nights thereafter, as the old woman's snores and the child's dry sobs combined in a rhythm of life-in-death and death-in-life, and life and death intertwined.

Valeria-Julia was terribly depressed this morning, as if she had been sewn into a thick cloth bag. It had happened again. It had been happening for all her life-- those stretches of time which she could not remember. Those blanks for which she could never account. What had happened last night? She could not remember anything beyond leaving the bakery and starting up the stairs to their rooms above.

Yet somehow, she had gotten to bed and awakened now, confused and troubled. She became aware that her hands felt sticky and unclean. She stumbled to the doorway. She held up her hands and gazed at them in the weak morning light. She gasped, horrified.

Her hands were coated with dry blood.

***

Old Marcella awoke in the middle of a monstrous snore. Awoke to pain. She had slept on her side again, and the leg on top, her bad leg, was gripped from hip to knee and held rigid by a cold, unendurable pain. The straw in the mattress was harsh against her fragile skin, and even the scent of the dried herbs mixed with the straw gave her no comfort. The pain was so deep in her bones that her gnarled hands could not soothe it with a warm touch or a gentle rub. She could not move, and she could not lie still. After an agonized moment, she managed to shift the leg to an easier position, and the pain lessened. She coughed a little, then lay quietly for a moment getting her stiff body accustomed to being awake. She blinked her sightless eyes a few times. In spite of all the years of blindness, she still had a momentary confusion upon waking in perpetual darkness.

Something was different this morning. Wisps of fear clung to her like cobwebs. Had she had a dream, or had something happened during the night? She shuddered without knowing why. Where was Valeria-Julia? Marcella vaguely remembered hearing the girl come in sometime in the dead of the night. Had she gotten up already and gone to her job at the bakery?

Marcella heard no breathing in the room except her own. Valeria-Julia was not there.

Marcella struggled to her hands and knees on the mattress and waited for the pain of first movement to subside or at least to become bearable. Then she pulled herself to the edge of the mattress and groping the stout stick that supported her and leaning on the wall, she got to her feet. She bent painfully and groped at the edge of the mattress for the clothing she had laid out the night before.

It was time to get to the temple for morning prayers and then to take her place among the beggars in the marketplace. She had a venerable position among the beggars. A merchant or perhaps another beggar would usually slip her a wedge of warm bread or something to drink, and during the morning hours shoppers or worshipers at the nearby temples would drop coins into her outstretched hand. Between Valeria-Julia's wages and what she, Marcella, could bring in, they lived reasonably well. At least they had shelter and were seldom hungry.

She blessed again, as she often did, the day when she took Valeria-Julia. Her own child, a son, had long since gone off with the Roman army and never returned. This little girl, an unwanted waif, whom neighbors called both Valeria and Julia, filled a great void in her heart. Not until Valeria-Julia could Marcella let go--though gently--the hope that her son would ever come back.

She had been a strange child, this little one. Marcella soon realized that in spite of her own advanced age and accumulated wisdom, this child, this half-twin was a puzzle. In the early days the child slept for long hours, ate hardly at all, and didn't even require washing and changing as babies usually did. It was as if she was still lingering between life and death. At night Marcella would hold the child to her shriveled breast and will her back to life until both would ease into slumber. Eventually, the child chose to live.

Something in Marcella knew that the healing of the wounds was not enough. There was a depth to this child that Marcella could never reach. Even as the burns sloughed off and were replaced by healthy flesh, and as cuts and bruises healed and faded, there were hurts that even Marcella's magic fingers could never reach. Marcella truly understood the child's fear of fire, for hadn't she been snatched out of the flames from death to possible life? But even as the child grew, there remained in her a solid core of fear. Early on, the little girl became frantic at the sight of flames, even small ones like the wispy little flames of candles flickering in the dark of night or choirs of candles in temples, calling people to worship. Valeria-Julia would curl up, knees to chin, and seem to shrivel into herself like a pork-rind in a too-hot fire. Marcella eventually took to undressing herself in the dark rather than to light candles; she even began leaving the little girl outside the temple while she herself went inside. As Valeria-Julia grew from toddler to little girl to bigger girl to almost-woman, the fear seemed to subside--or at least to stop being evident-- and Marcella was increasingly grateful to the gods for this child of her old age.

Still, Valeria-Julia was a puzzle. Even now, Marcella never knew whether she would be docile and gentle or rebellious and difficult. In spite of her devotion, Marcella could never penetrate a sense of aloneness which seemed to surround Valeria-Julia. But her strangeness made her that much more interesting. She had always seemed hungry for love--- starving--but unable to return love. Well, that was the way with young people, Marcella often told herself. And what child-- indeed, what person--could ever again, after so devastating an experience, be whole? So Marcella had nursed her through the early trauma, cleansing her wounds with healing herbs, calming her stormy emotions with chamomile tea and soothing massages, and salving her spirit with love and her own need for a child. Although Marcella had had some anxious moments, Valeria-Julia had been a blessing.

Now Marcella grasped the stick, its rough texture beneath her hand familiar and comforting. She stood for a moment waiting for the pain to subside. Then she groped her way to the water basin, which Valeria-Julia kept filled, and dipped in a cloth and began to wash. Going about the slow, aching ritual of getting up and getting dressed, Marcella found herself dwelling on past things. Dead things.

What was wrong with her this morning?

She remembered her early years as a slave in the Rufus kitchen. Her mother had been a slave in that household, brought from Egypt in her teens, who had grown into a tall brown woman with heavy hair black as midnight. They had been well-treated there. The master, of course, had slaked his lust on the young slaves and servant girls, and it was rumored that she, Marcella, was his daughter. It was possible. Her skin was brown like her mother's, but her nose was prominent and her eyes deep brown like the master's.

In any case, he had freed her when she was fifteen, along with her mother, and Marcella had gone to work as a cleaning girl and later a masseuse in the women's baths. Her hands were ever sensitive, and as she stroked and prodded and kneaded and tugged, her palms hot and reddened from the surge of spiritual energy, her hands told her things about her clients-- things about their lives, their feelings, their secret hungers, their tears in the dark of night. Lying naked beneath her healing hands, women confided their deepest thoughts.

Her hands found the spots where sickness would erupt, and sometimes she could advise them how to ward off disease. Her mother's teachings about healing herbs, and her own knowledge gleaned from long experience in the kitchen, were a decided asset. For Marcella, the mountain was the source of healing. The gods themselves had blessed it lavishly with soil that yielded the means to relieve suffering and bring joy. Trees, shrubs, flowers, even weeds, if one learned their secrets, could create miracles: They could sweeten the stomach, loosen the bowels or stop diarrhea, stem the flow of blood or bring on menstruation, cleanse wounds, make lovers mad with desire and prevent pregnancy or abort unwanted fetuses, perk up the depressed or calm the overexcited. Roots, stems, leaves or blossoms could be boiled, crushed, pounded, chewed raw, or rolled into capsules. In the compassionate hands of a skilled healer, plants growing wild on the mountainside, from the stately chestnut tree to the lowly knot grass, could bring joy and end pain.

Like gathering herbs on the mountainside, Marcella gathered bits of knowledge from the variety of people she encountered daily. She listened to them talk to each other in shops, on the street, in the baths. Sometimes they chatted with her, and she led them to contribute unawares to her cache of information. By piecing together the snippets, she began to know about the economy, politics, and even the history of their ancient city. She learned of the conquerors who had settled there, people who though long gone had left vestiges of themselves, traces that after centuries were still present. It was said that eons ago, even before the first whisper of history, the mountain had belched flames, and fiery vomit from the mountain's insides had poured down, burying trees and grass and animals and every living thing beneath burning rubble. The rubble, it was said, cooled, and in time became soil dark and rich and fertile, on which life grew again.

Still, Marcella learned, there were people who believed the old myth that giants lived in the pit of the mountain and would someday rise and wreak unspeakable havoc everywhere the mountain could reach. For some, then, in the very air that they breathed, there was a silent, invisible intake of fear.

Gradually her disparate pieces of knowledge and her psychic gifts coalesced into a solid core of wisdom. Gathering her healing herbs in the sunshine and shadows of the mountainside, Marcella often reflected how all of this life had grown from death-- how even death did not last forever.

As the years passed, Marcella earned a reputation as a healer and then as a soothsayer. She found that chewing laurel leaves intensified her gift of prophecy. Her swarthiness and the slight foreign accent from her mother endowed her with an air of mystery which seemed to enhance her image as a mystic. Some of the women even called her The Egyptian or The Mulatto. They felt that she was different from themselves, even the confidant of the gods, though not, of course, their social equal.

Eventually her hands began to weaken and to ache, and she left the baths. Her eyesight, too, began to narrow, like a circle slowly closing until there was only a pinpoint of light and then no light at all. She tried desperately to save her sight. She rubbed her eyes with an ointment of dried fennel juice and honey. But she could no more ward off the dark than she could prevent dusk from fading into night. Soon she could only remember the green of grass and trees, the blue and white of sky, the glory of sunrise, the majesty of the mountain which loomed over the city. Even now, after so many years, she cherished those memories, fixed like the frescoes on the walls in the homes of the wealthy. She frequently took them out of the recesses of her mind and examined them and reveled in them, then laid them gently away.

As her sight began to diminish, she began to develop a different kind of vision.

She could "see" things--occurrences from the past that nobody had told her about, or things that would happen in the future. She became a fortune-teller for the affluent and the wealthy, but she never denied her talents to the poor. By now she had Valeria-Julia, the child not of her body but of her heart. When her sight was truly impaired, the child would lead her to the rich houses and sit at her feet while she lay hands upon her clients and told them what the gods had revealed. The clients paid well.

***

Now, buffeted by memories, old Marcella groped her way to a stool in the corner and eased down wearily. She had a faint whiff of dried mint which they kept in corners to ward off beetles. She held her tired head in her hands. Why was she remembering these things today? And why were they so clear? She remembered, as if it were happening at this moment, that day in the heat of midsummer, with the warmth of the sun on her face, when she had had the vision.

She was never certain whether she had been asleep or awake. Perhaps it was a vivid dream that left her caught in its clutches. She hoped that it was only a dream. But deep inside, she knew that it wasn't.

On the day of the vision, she had gone to the temple as usual. The afternoon worship, the ceremony of the lustral waters had just ended. She was still enraptured, as always, with the profound joy of the ritual. Even in her blindness she could envision the priests and priestesses in their white linen robes; she could hear the whisper of their palm-leaf slippers. She could hear, too, and even feel the sprinkle of lustral water with which the priest blessed the worshipers; she could hear the rattle which another priest shook in honor of the goddess.

Still uplifted and reaffirmed, she groped her way to the temple steps, as was her custom. Her hands were now her eyes. Her fingers and palms knew every stone in the temple, and they guided her to the doorway and to the steps, where she would wait for the worshipers to disperse. Then she could more easily find her way home, for the sounds of people milling around distracted her, and sometimes she lost her direction.

On this day she had had a profitable morning. After the dawn service at the temple she had gone to the home of Julia Felix, surely the most wealthy woman in the city, telling the fortune of the house guardian's wife, seeing good things in that good woman's future. Perhaps Julia herself would be next, or the word would get out to her affluent friends. Julia knew some of the wealthy Roman ladies who had summer homes down by the seashore; she entertained them frequently. Perhaps she would mention the fortune-teller or even hire her for an evening's entertainment. Marcella's own future was looking hopeful. She lifted her face and felt the sun like a caressing palm.

Sitting primly on the temple steps, she thought with pride about how the congregation had rebuilt the temple, almost stone by stone, it seemed, since its complete destruction in the earthquake all those years ago. She was especially proud of Numerius Popidius Ampliatus, born a slave (she remembered his birth), who had achieved emancipation and made a fortune as a merchant; it was he who had financed the reconstruction of the temple. From a pile of rubble this gathering of the poor and the formerly poor had raised a splendid structure, not quite completed, a tribute to the ancient Egyptian goddess Isis, who had so blessed them all. A number of the wealthy had joined the temple, but to Marcella, Isis was still the goddess of the oppressed. Marcella's sensitive hands on the rough stone walls and the smooth columns reminded her of the temple's splendor. Now she opened her eyes wide to the sun, to the minuscule lessening of the darkness, which was as close as she would ever come to sight.

Then the babble of voices began to fade, smothered by a dull buzz like a ringing in her ears, and a faint aroma of bay leaves wafted around her. Her sightless eyes were dazzled by a rush of brilliant yellow light, and she gasped because she had not seen light for so long. The light flickered and writhed like fire or like a living thing in torment. The pleasant midsummer sunshine became scorching heat. A hot wind pummeled her, heat scorched her, and now rocks and liquid fire fell from the sky and covered her. A terrible hum rose and intensified to a roar, and she realized that the roar was the combined prayers and curses of people in torment. She tried to cry out, but her cries were stifled.

And now, above the shriek of the wind and the crash of falling rocks, she heard a voice.

At first she could not make out the words. But the voice became louder, rose above the cacophony. And the voice was hers.

...the explosion will rend the air and split your lives. Earth will shudder in horror beneath your feet, and at noon you will grope in midnight darkness. The mother will murder the child she has created. Sweat of summer will be on your brow, but you will tremble with winter's chill. Black rain will pour libations of poison upon you; stones and rocks will rise from earth and pelt you. Sea will recoil from you and rise

up before you, ready to pounce. The trembling mountain will vomit fire upon you. The mountain will move, the mountain will come to you. The air that you breathe will strangle you. Like ants you will scurry seeking shelter, but there will be no shelter. And the crazed gods, maddened by power, will scream with mirth at what their power has wrought, and then the gods will weep, horrified to behold the wanton destruction wrought by their own power.

All sounds stopped. The silence was more terrible than chaos.

Then the babble rose again: "...what's she saying?...what's wrong with her?...superstitious nonsense...too much wine...crazy old woman...no, wait, she knows things...crazy old woman...crazy..."

It was as if she had died and awakened to a new, terrible life. From that day, she was never free of fear. The vision haunted her like a persistent ghost. She could no longer tell fortunes: She could see only sudden violent death in anybody's future, and secrets buried under rubble. Nobody wanted to hear that. In desperation she took her place among the beggars in the marketplace. And she did well there. People gave freely, whether because of her age and blindness or because on some level of themselves they believed her prophesy of doom and were doing penance for denying her--whatever the reason, they gave freely. And she lived well, though uneasily. Because she knew what she knew.

II

Lucius the baker had far too much to do that morning to tarry in bed, although every instinct urged him to cuddle his wife's soft body closer, to explore again her secret places. But he was expecting deliveries of honey and berries from the mountain folk, and he had to send Tertius to the mill early to grind the corn. The Jacundus wedding was coming up, and he had to start on the bread and cakes.

Slipping into his sandals now, he glanced back to the hard bed where Augusta was still asleep on the fleecy white blankets. She lay on her side, the sheet hooked over her shoulder. Her breathing was peaceful as a baby's; her dark hair framed her face in wispy curls. She had a smooth little snore, more like a purr. Lucius stood uncertain for a moment. He should awaken her: His first wife Estella would have been up before him. She would be in the office downstairs organizing the day's orders or going over the accounts. But Augusta was young, hardly older than his youngest helper Valeria-Julia; he would have to mold her.

She sighed and rolled over on her back, one foot slipping out of the sheet. Approaching the bed to awaken her, he wanted instead to thrust his hand under the sheet and stroke her soft mound, feel her swell and grow moist under his touch, hear her murmur his name in her sleep.

Or somebody's name (the thought brought sudden sharp pain, which he squelched before the thought was completely formed) even if it wasn't his. He knew that she wasn't a virgin when he found her. How could a farm girl, beautiful and juicy, have escaped those lecherous farm boys? If, in the delirium of passion, she called out some name, it meant that he, Lucius, was satisfying her. And in some irrational way, the very pain spurred him on. Now, looking at her asleep, he was growing pleasantly hard. New life, new hope after the dry years with Estella. New beginning. New life.

He bent over her. Gently, so as not to awaken her, he fondled her breast. It was soft and voluptuous, the nipple hardening from her dawning pregnancy. Desire stirred in him sharply, and for a second he was tempted to lie down beside her and arouse her to the full heat of her passion, thrust his stiff penis into the warm wetness of her love, and ride her until their passion burst in a hot gush, and they cried out together. Yes, this time it could happen. But without waking she jerked away from his seeking fingers and turned petulantly onto her stomach. He smiled indulgently and a little ruefully, stroked her buttocks lightly, gave her breast a gentle squeeze, and turned away. Business called. Desire could wait. Business couldn't.

The old dog Dora was waiting outside the bedroom door. She limped painfully behind him, her hips stiff with arthritis. She was a little black dog of unknown ancestry, a bit overweight with advancing age. Her floppy dugs were testimony to her many litters of pups, unremembered and unmourned. Dora had been Estella's dog, unswerving in her loyalty.

The dog, in fact, had been the only object of Estella's gentleness. Since Estella's death four years ago, Dora had skulked around the house like a sullen ghost.

Dora whimpered. Lucius sighed and turned toward the atrium, the central hall from which the main rooms radiated. No time for old things, old thoughts. He felt again a rush of joy at the thought that Augusta would give him the child he had wanted from Estella, the child who, almost miraculously conceived, had killed Estella and itself. Augusta had been a farm girl, young and healthy. Surely--the thought flashed and faded like a bolt of lightning. No time for what-if's and maybe's. Deliveries to receive, grain to grind into soft white flour, workers to supervise, dough to knead, accounts to figure, plans to make for the Jacundus wedding. On an impulse he bent and stroked Dora's fuzzy head and whispered, "Go on back now, watch over your mistress." But he was dreaming again. There was no love lost between Augusta, who despite having lived close with animals on the farm, had an irrational hatred for this old dog, and Dora, who still considered Estella her mistress and had a deep antipathy for Augusta.

The servants--slaves and free--were waiting in the lararium at the shrine for the ancestors, for the brief religious ritual that started each day, a ritual of thanks to the gods and to the ancestors for Lucius' affluence that provided for them all, and an appeal for continued blessing. The lararium was a quiet little alcove near the kitchen, whose walls were bright with frescoes of mountain scenes teeming with life. In the middle of the alcove was a bust of Hercules, the city's collective ancestor, around which Lucius and his household--except, all too often, Augusta-- stood and offered their prayers. After the prayer the servants scattered to their respective duties.

His earlier thoughts of Estella made him pause and glance at the painting on the wall as he passed again through the atrium. The painting was a portrait of himself and Estella. It had been there for nearly twenty years, and after the first few days he had never bothered to look at it. But he felt an irrational compulsion to stop and peruse it now.

They had been young then, he and Estella, in their early thirties. There was still an innocence about them, although gazing at their images now, he perceived in her face--the set of her mouth, perhaps, or the way her hand clutched the account book, as if it were a part of her body--a shadow of the avarice that would both make and break them. Yet in youth their eyes were wide and dreamy. The bakery was starting to do well then, and between his artistry in the kitchen and her strong business sense, they were confident of success. And success had indeed come--at a terrible price. For as the years passed, they had grown in different directions, she toward business to the point of measuring the value of life itself in terms of profit and loss, he toward artistic creativity to the point of baking for the sake of art, not sales. Since her death he had had to become more oriented to business--but reluctantly.

Estella. When had she begun to change? The thought was new, even strange. In recent years he was accustomed to thinking of her as the abrupt, even cold, business-like Estella. But she had not always been so. Gazing at her face in the painting now, he suddenly recalled the warm, vibrant little person he had first loved. Love-making had been hot and passionate and joyful. He smiled now as he recalled that he had carved their names on the headboard of their first bed, a rough pine thing which her oldest brother had made for them. They had many a jolly romp and many a tender hour in that bed. What, he mused, had ever happened to that bed? What had they done with it when they moved into more affluent quarters? And when had she begun to change?

In the early years, he recalled, they had longed to have children. Every love-making had ended with the wish, spoken or unspoken, that this time there would be a baby. But month after month her flux would come. Then finally it happened. Their hopes soared as Estelle cheerfully suffered morning nausea and swollen, tender breasts. But somewhere in the third month, with no warning, the blood had gushed, and Estella was left as empty as their hopes. Was that when the change had begun?

No, not then. Because a few months later she was pregnant again, and their hopes burgeoned. This time Estella took numerous herbs to continue the pregnancy and offered special gifts to Venus. But again the pregnancy had ended in a rush of blood and pain. There were other disastrous pregnancies--he had lost count--and then there were no more. And one evening he discovered that she was taking rue seeds to prevent pregnancy. By now love-making had diminished and lost its joy.

The bakery became their child, and it flourished.

Well--memories didn't make money; hard work did. Resolutely, Lucius turned his back on the painting and brushed off the wispy touch of memory as one would brush a raindrop from his cheek. He hurried through the atrium into the vestibule. He smiled a little, as he often did, at the rich mosaic on the floor, depicting a dog who closely resembled Dora. Except that the dog in the mosaic had a rope around its neck, and Dora was too much of a personality for anyone to think of shackling her. Crossing the threshold on his way out, Lucius glanced at the little image which he, like most homeowners, had fastened to the doorway, in one form or another, to bring good luck. For Lucius' household, the tintinnabulum above the doorway made a cheerful sound as he opened the door. It was a silver replica of three bearded men with enormous, gracefully upward-curving penises from which hung little bells which tinkled when people entered or left the house. An assurance of prosperity and good fortune, a blessing from the gods. Lucius had a comfortable feeling that all was well. He smiled briefly and knowingly. Passing through the garden, he pulled a ripe peach from a low-hanging bough. He would have the peach and some bread and cheese when he got to the bakery.

Entering the street, he turned and looked back at his flower garden, the tinkling fountain, the fruit trees laden with figs and peaches and apples, the black marble table and chairs and the smooth stone couches for outdoor dining and lounging. He had ordered a bust of Bacchus from Greece to go beside the fountain. Who would have imagined, in his early years, that he would ever own such a house?

His thoughts crowded out a different reality. He did not hear Dora, crouched at the door as he left, whimpering.

He had done well, he and Estella. His house was not one of the biggest nor most lavish, but it was a world away from the house in which he had been born. His father had been a skilled worker in Eumachia's dye works. Even now, his rare thoughts of his father evoked the stench of dye and even the subtle hint of blue that clung to his father's skin. The old man had provided for his family simply but adequately. (Old man! He had been younger than Lucius was now, when he died suddenly and painfully, dipping fabric into the dye.) Well, none of that mattered now, Lucius reflected as he entered the street. He was so proud of his house--it was almost like an extension of himself. Although it had been Estella who brought the dream to fruition. Apprenticed to a baker, he learned the art and eventually married one of the workers in the same shop--Estella. They had lived in the shabby little apartment above the bakery. They had been happy in those days. Life stretched ahead of them, pregnant with promise. By the time the baker decided to move to Herculaneum, they (Estella) had saved enough money to buy the shop and the apartment. They worked hard and finally managed to buy a large old house on Abundance Way, one of the most fashionable neighborhoods. The move had been a great triumph.

But it had also meant a bend in the road, the kind of change in direction which one can realize only in retrospect, as now. A change not only in their residence but in themselves. After the miscarriages-- yes, after that--something in Estella's spirit hardened. More and more, Estella planned financial strategy to maintain the house and the business. She rented out

21

rooms in the house and became ruthless in dealings at the bakery. She began to seem less womanly to him. Estella was a tiny person, but the forcefulness of her personality and the firmness of her voice and gestures made her appear larger. Lucius began to feel intimidated by her; yet he enjoyed the new house and the new affluence which she had created. In her forties, without joy or passion, Estella conceived. But even as she fought off nausea and weariness, her furious pursuit of prosperity never diminished. This time, on a terrible day, the bleeding did not stop. Estella's hard-won affluence, Lucius now knew, had bought him Augusta.

He had plans for increasing the splendor of his home. He had servants to do what he himself in his early years had done for others. The Jacundus wedding would surely bring his bakery to the attention of the moneyed people, and he would have the means to create the fancy breads and cakes that so far existed only in his imagination. And now Augusta would give him a child! The future looked good. He breathed deeply, loving the feel of the early-morning sun on his skin. He did not notice that no birds were singing.

Lucius was enjoying his walk to the bakery. It was both relaxing and exhilarating, and it helped to keep him fit. Thinking of his new young wife, he was pleased (and a little arrogant) that he was more fit than most other men in their fifties. In spite of his thickening waist and thinning hair, he was still fit-- where it counted.

In the distance, the mountain growled. Lucius hardly noticed.

He ambled past the large, beautiful homes of the newly wealthy merchants and turned into Stabia Street toward the old commercial district. Now and then a cart would rattle down the cobbled street, and a few pedestrians made their way toward their place of employment. He waved at some of the walkers, and they waved back. They encountered each other every morning, and through their brief, almost surreptitious waves, they wished each other a good day. Passing one particularly splendid house, Lucius had to smile to himself: a slave was hurriedly folding up a colorful cloth which had been spread over a table in the yard, over yesterday's blazing sun, apparently as part of the festival for Vulcan, the god of fire, which had been celebrated yesterday. Passing the Stabian baths on the corner, Lucius anticipated an hour or so of relaxation there after lunch, in the heat of the afternoon. It was going to be oppressively hot today; he was sweating already. And the air didn't look exactly right. But having become a realist since Estella's death, he seldom asked why or how or what-if. What was, was.

He passed the Inn of Sittius and noted, as he always did, that the graffiti from the July elections were still there. Deep inside, he flinched a little, recalling the times when he himself had run for the office of aedile--and although he was successful, he still bore the scars of anger at some of the graffiti against him: One, especially, had claimed that he, Lucius, was a homosexual and an exhibitionist--no less than character assassination! Because he had not yet fathered a child, nor was he known to exploit his female servants, the socially sanctioned prey of the master. But he had ignored the accusation and actually won the election. He recalled with a sudden grin how his fellow-baker Caius Julius Polybus, running for municipal office, had been outraged when a prominent wall had proclaimed in huge red letters the scrawled endorsement of Caculla and Zmyrina, two prostitutes at a local pub.

Lucius smiled at a new bit of graffiti, apparently written last night, advertising the charms of a group of women, each of whom had her specialty: Palmyra the Oriental, Agglae the Greek, Maria the Jewess, Zmyrina the Exotic, and the lady who arranged their appointments, one Asellina. Lucius wondered about the nature of their specialties. Actually he had never felt at ease with prostitutes except in times of desperation. He was too afraid of the sickness prostitutes could bring, and he wanted the warmth of loving arms rather than commercial endeavors. But he did wonder about their specialties. Again he envisioned Augusta waiting for him on their bed, naked and eager. Pragmatist or not, his desires erased the boundary between dreams and reality.

He was optimistic and confident as he entered the courtyard to his bakery. Despite the stifling heat, he was walking a little faster now, because he was later than usual. But a quick glance told him that all was well. He rented out a portion of his facilities to other bakers; workers and slaves were scurrying around like ants in an ant-hill, grinding grain, shoveling loaves into the oven, and carrying all sorts of things here and there. Lucius was particularly proud of the oven. It was a large structure with an arched doorway, capable of holding up to eighty loaves. The oven, in fact, had been what finally convinced him and Estella, all those years ago, when they were shopping for their future, to buy this special bakery. Now, Lucius noted with satisfaction, slaves had fed wood into its monstrous craw. As Lucius approached, a slave shoveled in the last of the loaves and shut the iron door with a loud clang. The door, Lucius mused again, was made of lava from a long-ago eruption and then covered with iron. The previous owner had decorated the door with a travertine slab showing a raised image of a gigantic penis and the word "JOY." An earthquake had slashed a deep fissure in the door, splitting the bricks, the travertine image, and the JOY. But the oven still worked and turned out beautiful golden loaves. Lucius smiled to himself as he passed his outdoor counter and the little building which was the heart of the bakery. All was well. In another year or two, he promised himself again, he would look into expanding his bakery, buying a kneading machine, perhaps moving into larger facilities. He would have to buy several more slaves.

He was pleased that things seemed to be proceeding well this morning in spite of his tardiness. Yes, there was the slave Tertius, gathering bags of corn to take to the mill. But suddenly Lucius stopped in his tracks. There should be more loaves ready to go into the oven. His workers Statia and Petronia were frantically kneading and shaping the dough into rosette-shaped loaves. They were running behind time! Someone was missing. Lucius glanced around the bakery. "Where," he roared, "is Valeria-Julia?"

***

In one fluid motion, Augusta, waking, unwound from the little ball in which she had curled herself, and stretched luxuriously. The hard bed was covered with soft blankets and a layer of cool sheets.

Comfortable! She yawned, ending the yawn with a little sigh of contentment, and opened her eyes. Then she was instantly alert.

Lucius had gone. Good. It was probably fairly late. From the bustle she heard downstairs, the servants were well into their morning chores. That reminded her: She would have to prod Lucius to keep his promise to get her a maid of her own--someone to arrange her hair, which was thick and heavy, in the latest styles from Rome and Naples, someone to attend to her wardrobe and help her dress. Lucius was so slow about doing anything. Surely he could see that with her pregnancy, she needed a maid.

She was moving about the room now, her bare feet padding silently on the cool wooden floor. A little net of perspiration clung to her skin. Damn, it was hot already. She did miss the fresh morning breezes of the farm. And that was all she missed. She munched some grapes that Lucius had left in a silver bowl on the little table by the bed, hoping they would ward off morning nausea. Damn. She liked the idea of conceiving a child, but she hated the prospect of going through pregnancy. Reluctantly she slipped her feet into the sandals that she was expected to wear around the house. Draping a thin robe lightly around her, she headed for the toilet.

Damn that dog! As usual, Augusta almost tripped over the beast sprawled just outside her bedroom door. "Fat, funky old bitch! Why don't you go somewhere and die?" Augusta muttered. Dora lay there and stared at her malevolently. Augusta stepped over the stubborn dog and stalked--hurriedly now--to the latrine.

Back in her bedroom, Augusta felt a return of excitement and a sense of coming adventure. She had called one of the servants to take that disgusting dog downstairs and tie it up somewhere. Now, alone in the room, she flopped on the bed, flipped up her legs, and kicked her sandals high toward the ceiling, She giggled at the plop-plop as the sandals fell back to the bed. She spread her legs and liked the feeling. She relaxed and lay with her legs open. Then after a moment she sighed and sat up.

Time to get dressed. Well, she would certainly not wear that ugly stola that married women were supposed to wear. She would not even wear the loin cloth that both men and women wore as undergarments, nor the band that women wore. She didn't need any of that. Soon, dressed in a simple short blue tunic with a scarlet silk scarf just below her breasts, Augusta stood before her mirror and put the finishing touches on her rich dark hair. She combed it into swirls and curls, held it up off her neck with bright ribbons, snatched off the ribbons and let it fall around her shoulders and down her back. She loved her hair. When she was a tiny girl her older sisters used to play with her hair and dress her up like a little doll. She liked that. It made her feel special. Her mother was always working, either in the house or in the field, and had no time for her. Her father came in late, slumped at the rough wooden table, ate hungrily, then dropped into the one comfortable chair and snored every evening; she was admonished not to bother him. Both parents seemed to relate to the older girls, not to Augusta, the late and as she realized years later, the unwanted baby. After having all those girls, they had expected this surprise baby at least to be a boy and grow up to run the farm. Instead they had gotten Augusta.

She was the only pretty one of the girls-- everybody used to say so, and she could see that it was true. But as they grew up, her sisters began to resent her and even be mean to her, especially her oldest sister after their father died and the sister's husband took over the farm. Damn, Augusta didn't want her sister's ugly husband, even if he did keep looking at her with those pig-eyes of his! They began to keep her away as much as they could, sending her to town to help with the deliveries. Well, she didn't mind that. It was fun to get cleaned up and go flirt with the town boys. Their eyes caressed her, their desire made her--for the moment--whole. The farm folks were all relieved when the old and (to them) rich baker took to her, and she left and got married. She thought about them now, still on the farm, grubbing in the dirt and shoveling sheep-shit.

She giggled again and gave her hair one more swirl. She had washed it last night in a mixture of maiden-hair fern, wine, celery seed, and oil. Now it was thick and curly and glossy. Then she pushed it up on top of her head and fastened it with a clip studded with tiny pearls. Waves of dark hair cascaded down to her neck. She put one more dab of rouge on her cheekbones and closed her cosmetic box. She fastened a little gold necklace around her neck, calling attention to her high breasts and the soft blue of her tunic, and clipped long golden pendants onto her ears. She slipped her hand into her bracelet, a golden snake that slithered up her wrist. Her eyes were sparkling now in anticipation of her day; they were hazel-green and slightly slanted, with long thick lashes. She smiled broadly at her image in the shiny metal mirror. Yes, she looked fine.

She squeezed her feet into the heavy leather shoes that she needed to go into downtown. You never knew when you would walk into slime or piss or garbage or just plain murky water. Ugh! So like it or not, she struggled into the leather shoes.

She'd better go; she was already late.

She was going to meet her lover.

***

It was fully morning now. In his cramped room in the house of the actors, young Fabius lay sprawled on the cot in his tiny cubicle, not about to awaken to the new day. He lay on his stomach, his right arm and leg dangling over the side of the bed. In a more graceful position, he might have resembled a nude Greek statue of a victorious young athlete, well-muscled and beautiful. His eyes were wide open, his mouth agape as if in surprise. He was not about to awaken. Ever.

***

Valeria-Julia was stumbling by now, her breath coming in short gasps. Her legs felt weak, as if they could no longer hold her. Each breath was a painful gasp. She longed to collapse under a tree and be cradled by the grass and the immovable earth. But panic spurred her on. Still wearing the tunic, stiff now with dry blood, she had fled out of their rooms above the bakery, through the quiet early-morning streets, past the neat houses with the lush summer gardens and gurgling fountains, past the silent shops, and now out beyond the city into the suburbs, toward the Gate of Vesuvius. She was fleeing to the mountain, which had ever been her refuge. But first she had to travel through the necropolis--the city of the dead.

She was staggering by the time she reached the gate. She hesitated for a moment at the arch which was the boundary between the living and the dead, beyond which stood the mountain. She sank to the ground beneath the arch and laid her head against its cool stone. She was trembling, and the earth trembled, too. She crouched there until her breathing became slow and even. Then she got up and stepped through. On the other side, she turned and glanced back. At the top of the arch she noted, as if for the first time, the name of the city, chiseled in immutable stone: POMPEII.

III

Above the city, majestic and mighty, loomed Vesuvius. Ubiquitous mountain. There was no part of Pompeii where Vesuvius was not felt. The city rested between the mountain and the sea. From the farthest reaches of the Roman world on giant ships the sea had brought them wealth and wisdom. And Vesuvius, hovering over them, had protected them from the storms and nurtured them with rich farmlands, grazing lands, woodlands, and a sense that the gods lived there. Surely Dionysus lived there, providing grapes for the wine which had made their city famous, and Venus, their patron, goddess of love and beauty must have made beautiful Vesuvius her home. The lowing cattle, the breezes scented with pine and wildflowers, the rustling of leaves, the clean smell of fresh-turned earth, the merry songs of the birds, the sight of grain waving in sunny fields, ruddy-cheeked children running along the roadsides--poets and painters were not alone in their praise of Vesuvius. Yes, surely Vesuvius was the dwelling place of the gods. Pompeii, nestling at its base, was blessed.

Valeria-Julia had passed through the gateway from Pompeii into the the city of the dead. Here rested the ashes of the city's ancestors. Stone monuments, splendid with bas reliefs, statues, and columns, rose from the ground, reminding the living of the affluence of the honored dead and reaffirming that death was imminent and pleasure should not be postponed. Jars and amphoras containing ashes of slaves and servants stood around ornate vases containing the revered ashes of their masters, the slaves and servants still, apparently, ready to serve. Yet shops lined the road, as if life could not relinquish the dead, or perhaps the dead could not relinquish life.

Over everything, the scents of death hovered like a cloud--not the stench of rot, since the flames had cleansed the decay of the flesh, but the lingering perfume of funeral spices, wilting flowers and stale remnants of wine and oil.

Dawn had broken, and shopkeepers were already beginning to set out their wares. But nobody noticed Valeria-Julia, driven by desperation; it was as if she were invisible.

Still exhausted, Valeria-Julia wandered into the mourning room of a particularly ornate tomb. The walls were covered with paintings of birds and gentle animals and flowers and green trees, all alive with vibrant colors. A long table in the middle of the room had obviously held lavish feasts in honor of the revered departed, feasts in which the mourners ate and drank to satiety. Three stone couches surrounded the table, couches which must have once been covered with soft blankets and even furs but were now bare. Valeria-Julia entered the welcoming dimness of this room. She sank down on one of the couches, trying to control her panic. The stone couch was cool after the oppressive heat outside.

She had to sort out this terrible thing. The necropolis had ever been her sanctuary. There she could be alone with eternity. She lay curled up, knees to chin, eyes closed, her thumb in her mouth. What had happened? What had she done?

She clung to a dead baby, slippery with blood, and the dead baby was herself.

***

Marcella, fully awake now, was still caught between memories, troubled dreams, and uneasy reality. She cried out again for Valeria-Julia, but her voice was like the sound of rose petals dropping onto soft soil. In rising panic, she limped around the room, losing herself among familiar objects, groping and grasping, lost. She dropped her stick and had to cling to the walls. "Where are you?" she kept calling into the emptiness. "Little one, where are you?" Until finally the arthritic limbs collapsed, and she sank into a strange and unfamiliar corner and whimpered without words. For she knew. Now she knew. In this strange, familiar, empty, haunted room, her blind eyes saw fragments of her long-ago vision. And she knew.

This was the day that would bring tears to the eyes of the gods.

***

"Three!" Statia was saying. "I've seen twins--but three!" She had stopped kneading and was just standing there, her hands buried in dough up to her wrists.

Petronia, obviously enjoying her role as the bearer of good gossip, never broke her rhythm as she shaped and patted the loaf she was fashioning. "Born just before the festival of Vul..."

"Dammit, where is Valeria-Julia?" fumed Lucius, bursting into the cubicle. Petronia and Statia jumped, startled by Lucius' sudden appearance. "We don't know," said Petronia as respectfully as she could under the circumstances. "She's hasn't come in yet. We've got to do her work until she gets here."

Lucius cursed again, grumbled, and went about setting things right.

He was not ordinarily a cursing man, but the heat of the day and the pressure of the heavier-than-usual workload made him irritable. And he had not had a chance to eat his bread and cheese and fruit. The smell of freshly-baked bread made him hungrier and stoked his irritability. "These young girls," he muttered, "...wrong time of the month, all they want to do is sit home and suffer." He was being unfair, and he knew it. Young as she was--barely nineteen--she was a mainstay of the business. Quiet and efficient, she saw to things--saw that deliveries were received and put away, that the other workers--all older than she--were going about their chores, that customers were served and, on rare occasions, mollified. Even the slave Tertius liked her; his customary scowl relaxed a little in her presence, and Lucius knew that in their few idle moments, they talked--about what, Lucius had never wondered. Tertius was inclined to be troublesome and even rebellious, but his friendship with Valeria-Julia seemed to soften him. Now, that was another source of irritation this morning: Tertius. Why was he always surly and angry?--not at all like Lucius' docile domestic servants. Lucius was kind to him, fed him and clothed him adequately. Tertius lived well for a slave. What did he have to be angry about? Some slaves, Lucius knew, aspired to emancipation; some later became wealthy, influential men. Why did Tertius have to be so resentful? Lucius' customary good humor was gone.

He had been wrong about Tertius. Ruefully, Lucius recalled the morning when he had bought Tertius. Lucius had gone to the slave market to look over the fresh supply of slaves, hoping to find a sturdy male to do menial work around the bakery. Perhaps he would be lucky enough to find one who had the intelligence to work his way up to more skilled tasks. Estella had usually gone with him to these transactions, but Estella was dead now, and Lucius was on his own. He spotted Tertius on the revolving platform on which slaves were displayed for prospective buyers. Most of the slaves were naked, so that customers would see what they were getting. Some slaves had placards around their necks with whatever information was necessary. Tertius' placard warned that he had a rebellious nature; he would be sold cheaper because of that. At first Lucius did not even consider him. Tertius' head was up, and he gazed at prospective buyers in a way that Lucius found disturbing. Estella would never buy such a slave. But the image of Tertius, naked, chained, and no longer young, somehow stayed with him, and by the time Tertius revolved again, Lucius was convinced that their eyes locked. Lucius knew that he was a kind master who could tame Tertius' need to rebel and that Tertius might have the spirit and the intelligence to be an asset to the bakery. And besides that, he would be a good financial deal, being fairly inexpensive.

On the third time around, Lucius bought Tertius. Altogether, Lucius thought, a good bargain. He had been wrong.

"Tertius!" Lucius bellowed now, years later, "Get the mule out there to the mill. The morning's half gone already." That was an exaggeration, of course, but he felt a terrible anxiety, as if he were pursued by time, which was rapidly running out.

Tertius looked up from the tray of loaves he was about to carry across the courtyard to the white-hot brick oven. His glance was filled with seething hatred; his silence as deadly as rattlesnake venom. He carried the loaves out to the oven and shoveled them inside, then started over to the pen where Lucius' mule was kept. It was past time to grind the grain.

"TERTIUS!" Petronia's sharp voice pierced the air. "Come and get these loaves!"

Tertius glowered toward the cubicle, his eyes gleaming beneath his heavy brows. "I've got to get the mule to the mill," he called, heading for the mule's pen. "The master says so." He almost collided with a farmer coming into the courtyard with two enormous baskets of eggs.

The bakery was one of several that faced outward onto a courtyard which was ringed with the necessities of their trade--two or three mills for grinding grain, a large oven or two, and across the court from Lucius' place, a stable where the more affluent bakers kept their mules.

Heading across the cobblestones to the stable to get Lucius' mule, Tertius frowned and moved faster than usual, propelled by nervous energy. He was worried about Valeria-Julia. It wasn't like her to be late. Even with her changes in mood, changes in personality, she was always there to do her job. He had planned to slip the loaves in the oven and then, if she had not appeared, to climb the stairs to her rooms--hers and old Marcella's--and find out what was wrong. Because surely something was wrong. He felt it. He had seen her leave the house last night, hurriedly, almost frantically, and he had worried then. Her face was tense, her movements jerky. She was going to meet Fabius--he was sure of that. Damn that Fabius! Tertius had tried to stay awake until she returned, but sheer physical exhaustion had overcome him. Had she come home at all? Damn!

Tertius crossed the courtyard, crowded with slaves and servants shoveling newly-formed loaves into the ovens, pouring grain into the tops of the mills, pushing the long handles that turned the mills and ground the grain. Most of the workers were slaves, their skin bronzed by the sun, most in worn sandals but some barefoot, clad in ragged short tunics with slave-belts around their waists. Some nodded briefly at Tertius, but most simply continued their labors.

Tertius was one of the lucky ones: Lucius had a mule, whose strong shoulders and muscular legs did the work that other bakers' slaves had to do. Tertius entered the stable and found a measure of comfort in the scent of animals, natural and uncomplicated. He pulled the mule from his stall. The ungainly beast gazed at him with soft brown eyes. "Come on," whispered Tertius. "Time to work."

In spite of his irritation over a bad start this morning, Lucius greeted the egg man warmly. Cornelius, the egg man, had a farm on the mountainside and had delivered fresh eggs to Lucius (and Estella) for years. A loose relationship had developed. "So how are things going for you, Cornelius?" Lucius asked after they had concluded their business in the cubicle. Lucius was walking with him back to his wagon, where the skinny little mule was waiting patiently.

"All right, I guess." Cornelius, settling himself again in the wagon, wiped his face on a handy rag. "Hens aren't laying well; I'm not going to deliver all my eggs today. But that happens now and then. Hot today, isn't it? I'll see you next time." Cornelius turned the wagon, and headed out of the courtyard.

Lucius turned back to the cubicle, where Petronia and Statia were already preparing the next batch of loaves. Valeria-Julia had still not come. "Dammit," said Lucius again. "Where *is* Valeria-Julia? Petronia, go upstairs and see if she's there, and tell her to come down right now!" Where was Valeria-Julia? WHY IS SHE NOT HERE? Petronia hurriedly washed her hands, glanced at Statia, whose fingers were flying as she kneaded the next batch of dough, and started outside toward the rickety stairway.

Lucius had to hustle to take care of his business. Two more deliveries to come: honey from the beekeeper and a pewter jug of Vesuvinum, the wine for which Pompeii was famous, from the winemaker. The winemaker came first to bring the Vesuvinum. Actually the Vesuvinum was for Lucius' personal use, his and Augusta's. He would take the jug home, and in the evenings he and Augusta would sip wine from Estella's crystal goblets, and he would tell Augusta all the things that weighed heavily on his heart. This time it would happen that way, he knew it would. She would listen silently and let him hold her close, and he would be overwhelmed by her nearness and her lemony scent. As the wine flowed and he talked on, she would move closer to him and she would lay her head on his shoulder and breathe deeply as he talked about the dreams of his youth and he would become young again, with the fulfillment of all his hopes still ahead. Then he would lead her into the bedroom, and the years would melt away and he would be young, not with youth as he had actually lived it, which was drab and filled with hard work and little pleasure, but with the youth of his dreams. He would be handsome and virile, transformed by her love.

These thoughts flashed through him and disappeared, leaving no trace except a slight twinge of an erection as he set the jug in a corner by the entrance. The counter was open now, and customers had started to drift toward it, outside the doorway. Where was Valeria-Julia? She did have days, he remembered now, when she seemed different--abrupt, impatient, distracted, almost like somebody else. Maybe this was one of those days. But she had always been here, even so.

He had been in such a good mood when he left his house and strolled the quiet streets of the awakening city. But as soon as he got to the bakery his day had started to unravel. Increasingly he had a feeling of unease. Something was wrong, and he was too busy to stop and figure it out.

***

"Maybe she's getting ready to die or something," suggested the servant boy. "She's acting really weird this morning."

The dog Dora was causing problems. At Augusta's insistence, they had shut her up in the room of the house guardian, Longinius, but had freed her as soon as Augusta went outside into the garden. Now in spite of her age and infirmities, Dora was wandering restlessly from room to room, turning up unexpectedly underfoot, whining, scratching at doors. As the morning wore on, her pace accelerated to a creaky desperation. The whines became plaintive yelps. Now she had wandered to the vestibule where she stood at the front door.

Longinius knelt in front of her and took her face in his hands. "What's wrong, girl? A little off-center this morning?" Dora whined softly and gave three or four piercing barks. Longinius glanced up at the boy. "Seems like she's trying to talk. Look at her eyes. She's got a story to tell."

Dora broke loose and resumed her frantic odyssey toward the atrium. Her toenails clicked a rapid staccato on the tiles. Her breath came in harsh gasps.

"See what I mean? Weird."

"Better put her back upstairs in my room." Since Estella's death, Dora had drawn closer to the house guardian and often slept at the foot of his bed. "Maybe she'll calm down."

The servant boy trotted after Dora, who was limping badly now. He caught her by her leather collar and began pulling her toward the stairs. With

40

surprising strength, she resisted, yelping in sudden pain.

"Hey, not like that!" Longinius snapped at the servant boy. "Come on, girl, come with me." He bent and stroked her head. Then he led her gently by the collar. She followed, her tail wagging nervously.

***

Leading the slow, apparently placid mule, Tertius trudged around and around the millstone, grinding the corn. Around and around in endless circles. He and the mule. Grinding corn for the master. Corn for the kind master. The kind master. Around and around.

The thick leather belt inscribed with the name of his owner, which Tertius, like all slaves, wore, was heavy and unbearably hot The mule wore a halter, and Tertius wore a slave-belt, and they both trudged around and around the mill, grinding corn for the kind master. Endless circles. Circles of the mind.

He had always been a slave. He had never been a slave.

The fire of freedom still burned brightly within him, despite the attempts of a succession of "masters" to smother it. The beatings had left his wrists scarred from rope burns and the skin on his back rumpled up, swollen like a swarm of starving snakes on the hunt. A lash across the face had left an angry scar from his cheekbone to the corner of his mouth, giving him a perpetual one-sided smirk. The constant threat of torture had encapsulated fear inside him, fear which grew with time and threatened to break out of the capsule in which he had imprisoned it and spread its poison into every cranny of his being. Worst of all was the scar upon his soul--the loneliness. For he had learned when he was a child, on that bright summer morning when they had torn him from his mother's grasp, jammed him into a cart with other wailing or silent slaves, and sped along the cobbled streets to the city of Rome, that a slave was adrift in a hostile world--alone, without ties to anyone except the master. He learned this from his mother's screams and his own. His memories of his mother were fragmentary now, seldom rising to consciousness: The scent of sweat on a woman worker, the moan of the wind in the trees, the touch of rough cloth on his cheek, brought quick pain which he thrust back into the morass of the unremembered. The memory of their parting and the terrible alone-ness afterward had plunged so deep inside that it could never be exhumed. Not even now, as he trudged behind the recalcitrant mule, dredging up the long-dead, will it or not.

The lesson was reinforced through the years as he was sold from place to place, from master to master, as he saw the things he saw--men and women and sometimes children beaten to a broken and bloody mass as a warning to others who, like them, might be tempted to steal food; women forced to the master's will, whose cries--when they had the spirit to cry out--seared the souls of those who heard; families shattered like crystal under a hammer.

When one is truly alone, the soul shrivels into a small, hard thing like a peach pit, rotted inside.

It was a bitter lesson. There were times when he had reached out to someone, often to a woman whose tenderness was balm. But he learned that a slave had no right to love, only to lust. A woman and a child had taught him that. So he had tamed even lust. His fierce celibacy was a weapon. There were times when his body rebelled against this furious abstinence. His palms longed to caress soft flesh, his fingers to probe a woman's hidden places. And in spite of his mind's stern command, his penis swelled, desperate for a woman's moist warmth. In the early years after Clara, he had quenched his lust on whatever woman was willing. But as his spirit closed down, even that human contact became threatening. In night's nadir, lying in the slave- room of a master's house or on the bed of rags on the floor of the bakery, his seeking fingers clutched his own swollen member and pumped and pumped until the spasm, the groan, when his seed spilled out on the rags and his tortured body finally found relief. But there was no relief for his deepening rage.

Around and around in endless circles, grinding corn for the master. He and the other beast of burden.

THE DAY THE GODS WEPT

IV

Augusta was enjoying breakfast in the garden. She loved dining outside at the black marble table and chair, their smooth beauty gleaming in the morning sun. She loved ordering servants to bring her whatever she chose, sitting back and being served. (She could speak to them in Oscan, the language of the long-ago conquerors, which everyone had spoken on the mountain; here, people tended to speak the language of Rome, and she was not entirely at ease with it.) In the old life, when she was toiling barefoot on the farm, who would have thought that she would ever, ever have all of this? Why, Lucius even had slaves! On the farm they had never had slaves. She and her sisters and their mother had worked like slaves just to keep the place going. Now she gazed happily around the garden at the marble fountain in the center, the profusion of flowers in full bloom in lush beds around the borders, the luscious fruit hanging from the trees. The still air was heavy with the perfume of the flowers and ripening fruit.

Well, she had earned it. She was good to Lucius. She made him happy, and that was what counted. When he touched her and she knew what was coming, her mind would erase him and in his place would be some boy she had known in the fields or barn, or more recently, her lover. And she would open and moan and lock her legs around Lucius' wide back, and when it was over and she had to return to time and place, she was at least assuaged though not satisfied.

Settling back in the marble chair, Augusta sipped her milk and munched the chunk of bread from Lucius' bakery. The morning was hot. And there was something else, something indefinable. In spite of her current status as a city lady, she was at heart a farm girl, and something in her felt that nature was out of kilter. The scent of laurel and chamomile was soothing. But the air was strangely silent and--what?-- stifling. She realized with a shock that there was no riot of birdsong, no chirping or calling to each other from tree to tree.

But she didn't dwell on this oddity. She had other things to think about--to feel. Absently, she took a bite of fruit, a peach right off the tree, as she had ordered. The peach was sweet, its rich juice filling her mouth and lingering on her lips, which she licked and then blotted delicately with a soft napkin as she had seen the city ladies do. She gazed briefly at the peach tree above her, bursting with golden fruit framed by glossy deep-green leaves. She had watched the fruit grow from bud to blossom to hard little lumps and finally to luscious peaches which the tree yielded easily to a touch. She took another bite. The flesh was soft but firm on her tongue. She sucked the sweet juice.

She was in no hurry. Her lover would have to wait. The anticipation, even the irritation, would be good for him. Would heighten his passion.

Oddly, it did not heighten hers.

The feeling persisted that there was something strange about this morning. All those years had sensitized her to the rhythms of nature, and now a subtle feeling which had begun in her depths was starting to rise to her conscious self: Something was wrong. The sun was sparkling down upon them, making bright patterns between the leaves of the fruit trees, but it seemed unnaturally hot for this early in the day. And no birds flitted from tree to tree. No birds sang. The silence was discomfiting. Not natural.

Her eyes wandered to the sun dial. Usually she loved that sundial: it was beautiful in the sunshine, its shadows black against the glowing bronze. But today it made her uncomfortable. Yes, she was late for her date with her lover. Probably that was why she had an unaccustomed sense of urgency. Well, she wasn't going to rush. She took the last bite of her peach.

Perhaps the strangeness of the summer day prodded loose other thoughts and feelings that she had squelched. Why was she not hurrying to meet her lover? Was it because of her pregnancy?--because her restless body was now fulfilled?--because the cycle of nature would finally be completed? She had not wanted to be pregnant. She had drunk a foul-tasting water in which she had boiled wormwood and juice of rue. But in spite of the potion's bitterness, the pregnancy had gone merrily on.

For years she had not thought of that other baby. The child who, for her, had never lived. Never really become a child. She had been so young--barely in her teens, barely away from the dolls that her father had fashioned for her from rags and feathers. She had surrendered to the blandishments of some farm boy and to the insistence of her ripening body. Then the body had taken over. She missed her monthly flux. The body had become her whole self. It made her vomit, demanded that she eat and pee frequently at odd times, swelled in gross proportions. Her mother and even her father turning from her, aiming new anger at her--another mouth to feed--her sisters openly disgusted. Her fearful isolation. Then that awful morning, the agony, and her guttural cry like that of a tortured animal, and then the sudden release, the baby's single lusty cry, then silence. Dead, they told her later, but she had never, in her deepest self, felt death. Her body, flushing out fluids from her most intimate parts-- blood, milk wasted--as if purging the reality of what had happened, and her mind purging the memory. Until this strange morning.

Augusta closed her eyes and let her mind wander back to several days ago, nearly two weeks!--to her last visit with her lover. She had brought him a gift--a soft blanket to spread over the hard couch on which they would lie. (A gift to her own comfort, really.) Later on that day, walking home and not even feeling the lumpy cobblestones beneath her feet, she had wondered whether he would wash the blankets before he laid the next woman.

***

Valeria-Julia awoke as from a deep slumber, her thumb still in her mouth. She sat up and sniffed the heavy air. She was in the city of the dead. She struggled up, her young muscles aching from the harshness of the stone monument on which she had been sleeping. The heat was suffocating; her hair hung limp and damp on her forehead, and her legs were slippery with sweat. The ground was hard and dry; the dry grass crunched beneath her feet. Cypress trees lined the walkway, looming tall and slender and menacing above her. No birds sang. The world was immersed in an ominous silence.

Fabius. He was ever on her mind, lingering near the surface, but today his image was more than usually persistent. Frightening. There was something she was supposed to remember.

She had both loved and hated Fabius for all of her life. The love came first. Her earliest memory of Fabius--or what became fixed in her mind as memory, though it might have been a dream--was the summer afternoon when Marcella had gone to tell his mother's fortune. Valeria- Julia remembered the lush garden where they had waited, the blue and yellow flowers that perfumed the breeze. It had rained, and the air was fresh. She was tired from the long walk. Marcella had been out of sorts, urging her to walk faster and not letting her stop and sniff the people's flowers. As they waited on the stone bench, the little girl looked with delight at the garden around her. When the lady came to greet them, a boy scampered at her side. Valeria-Julia did not like boys. They teased her and laughed at her scar. But as soon as she saw this boy, she loved him.

His hair was bright, lit by the sun, his head encircled by light. He was smiling--not laughing at her. This part of the memory was vivid; she could always conjure up this first vision of Fabius. They were the age when children begin losing their baby teeth. She had lost her front teeth, but he still had his.

In later years when she closed her eyes and sank into this memory, she thought that between the scar on her forehead, her thin dark hair, and her lack of front teeth, she must have been an ugly sight. But he was a young god, sturdy and confident and beautiful. While his mother and Marcella talked, they played in the garden amid the sweet-scented flowers and apple trees. She could never remember what they did, but she never forgot that when it was time for her to go and his mother said, "Tell the little girl goodbye," he planted a wet kiss on her cheek. Her face flushed hot, and she stood there not knowing what to do. Marcella and his mother had laughed and said that he was so cute. But the kiss roared through her entire being. It sealed her future. And his.

As they grew, they encountered each other many times--in shops, on the streets, sometimes in his parents' house when Marcella returned occasionally to tell fortunes. Waiting for Marcella inside the house was intimidating. The house was huge. Once, early on, her curiosity had overcome her timidity, and she wandered from the reception room where they had put her to wait, and got lost in the maze of rooms and the crush of people who were rushing about, too intent upon their own concerns to notice the lost little girl. Fabius had found her cringing in a corner. He laughed and she felt stupid and ashamed until he took her hand and led her back to where she was supposed to be. She felt secure with her hand in his, going willingly where he led.

Yet some small part of her resented his authority and wanted to snatch her hand from his and find her way on her own.

As she grew older she began to feel smothered by the busyness of the house. It wasn't only the number of people moving through--tenants, family members, clients, servants, slaves--but the way the house was furnished. Walls were covered with pictures, floors had elaborate mosaic designs, statues lurked in every room. Marble tables were filled with silver bowls, gold candlesticks, carved wooden birds, implements of all kinds. Bronze lamps were everywhere, and sconces on the walls held fat candles. Once she waited in the kitchen while Marcella told the fortunes of some of the dinner guests. Valeria-Julia huddled on a stool against the wall while servants and slaves rushed about preparing more food than she had ever seen in one place--game roasted crisp brown, even roasted mice stuffed with mint and herbs, oysters and shrimp arranged around enormous baked fish, apples and grapes and peaches piled high in silver dishes, bread of all kinds stacked on platters, dazzling amphoras of wine. In the dining room the long table, its ebony wood glistening, the scent of the food blended with the perfume of flowers freshly cut and the gentle smoke from the candelabra. The little girl's mouth watered for the food, but her stomach churned with tension. Fabius was somewhere helping to entertain his mother's guests.

Valeria-Julia was never comfortable in that house. The only quiet place was the garden where she had first met Fabius when they were mere tadpoles and she had no front teeth. But this house was Fabius' world. He belonged here. He glowed here like a gem in the flicker of the living fire from the torches that lined the halls.

After Marcella had the vision and stopped telling fortunes, there was no need for Valeria-Julia to be in Fabius' house. By then she and Fabius were in their teens, and Fabius--a boy and a privileged one at that-- was increasingly free to run the city streets.

Valeria-Julia had a way of unconsciously watching for him, certain that in the most unexpected moments he would appear. And often he did. Sometimes they would saunter off to the mountain and sprawl on the coarse grass. They might loll beneath a walnut tree and toss nuts at the squirrels or munch tart wild apples. Birds called from tree to tree and sometimes broke out into glorious song as if they could not contain their exuberance. Scarlet valerian flowers cascaded over rocks and fallen trees, and patches of wildflowers were a soft mosaic of color. There alone with Fabius, Valeria-Julia was filled with quiet joy; some restlessness in her was, for the moment, at peace.

As the years passed, their friendship continued to ripen. She learned that his father made money selling houses, for the earthquake that had destroyed her family and charted her life's direction had created opportunities for others to prosper. Fabius had a tutor, but not being inclined toward learning, he brought his lessons to Valeria-Julia, and she learned them and she taught him. He was not an easy pupil even for her. He preferred play-acting with stout sticks as swords, making eloquent though incomprehensible speeches as he vanquished her.

A latent interest in learning began to stir in him at age thirteen or so when his parents took him with them to see a play at the Small Theatre. It was a comedy with all sorts of crazy goings-on. In the midst of the crowd, laughing and applauding, Fabius was transfixed. He became each of the characters--the handsome hero, the smug landowner, the slave turned trickster, even the beautiful heroine and her crafty maidservant. Fabius knew--even though he could never put it into words--that his real self was not in the audience watching passively as life paraded before him, but on the stage creating life as it was and as it could be.

He left the theater different from the little boy brought by his mother to be shown off to her friends like another ostentatious piece of jewelry. He was too young, of course, to know that life-altering changes can occur in unobtrusive moments unnoticed and that from this time he trod a different path.

Yet his new direction diverted only a little from his old path, as if the passion of all his life had merely anticipated and fed into the new. As a little boy he had developed a deep admiration for athletes, and he dreamed of being a wrestler or a discus-thrower or, ultimately, a driver in the chariot-races. Hero-worship became a passion, fed by the afternoons at the amphitheater watching the games with his father, whose stern face relaxed into smiles, and whose restrained voice roared into cheers and shouts for a triumphant athlete. The child Fabius saw himself on the field eliciting that same fervor, and in his play-acting, he was a combatant ever undefeated. Even as he matured and the fantasy faded, the residue remained, and he routinely went to the Palaestra, just outside the amphitheater, first to watch the athletes work out and then, as he grew older and bigger, to work out with them, building his muscles and honing his body to be a sharp, efficient instrument. And his body became beautiful – well-muscled, well-proportioned, and golden. An athlete's body. An actor's body.

His dream to become an athlete was replaced by his ambition to become an actor, but he continued his workouts. He loved the intensity of competition, an intensity which blotted out everything else but the present moment and the task at hand. He loved the warm glow afterward and the smell of his own sweat, and the relaxation of the subsequent bath and massage. He emerged from the bath glowing with health and ready for adventure.

Early on, Fabius and Valeria-Julia had realized that boys were different from girls, and whenever the opportunity arose, they experimented, first with showing, then with touching, then with awkward stroking and caressing. One afternoon when they were in their teens, they wandered to the mountain, and in the bushes on the soft sweet grass, fully clothed and overcome with unaccustomed shyness, they coupled.

After that, she took to sex with unexpected wantonness, her appetite matching and sometimes even exceeding his. Yet she was never quite satisfied, as if she were seeking something indefinable and elusive. She confused and frustrated him. Sometimes she burned with desire; sometimes she was distant and in some part of herself, chaste. Sometimes, when he saw her a few days afterward and whispered in her ear, she seemed not even to remember their encounters. She was often quiet and submissive, as he thought a woman should be, but sometimes she had violent outbursts of temper, which he met with patronizing humor. He never knew quite what to make of her. She was confusing but also fascinating.

As her body and spirit grew, so did her love for Fabius. But even in her early years, she came to know that he could not return her devotion. She had a deep need for love and acceptance, but he did not. Everyone admired him, including and especially girls, and for him that was enough. He enjoyed life. And life was going well. Whatever his relationship with other women, it was to Valeria-Julia that he confided his ambitions to become an actor, and she was the one whom he sought out to tell of his progress.

"I got a part!" he boasted to her one afternoon, leaning on the counter in the bakery. "Hey, I got a part in a play!" It was not a major role--in a skit by a local writer, he was a soldier who simply had to stand around looking menacing. But it was a beginning. The sight of the crowds of people in the audience, the roar of applause at the end of the play--these things fed a hunger in him that he had never been able to define but that had always tantalized him and would never be satisfied but would forever hold him captive.

And he rushed to tell Valeria-Julia. She rejoiced with him. She had never seen a play, but she knew from his enthusiasm that this was for him a milestone. He came back later that evening, and they went to the mountain where they had played as children, where they had shared their feelings and their secrets. And what he had learned from other women he brought to her, and he taught her. He caressed her with gentle fingers, and with eager lips and tongue, he kissed her all over, all over. And although she didn't know the word itself, she knew the meaning of ecstasy.

His first speaking part was another triumph. Playing a servant in a comedy by the playwright Menander, he had only two or three lines, and he was so overcome by stage fright that he fumbled even those. But he must have done something right, because afterward his fellow-actors, experienced in the art of theater, told him he had done a good job and said that they hoped to work with him again. So he sought out Valeria-Julia, and they celebrated. It never occurred to them that she should come and see the next play.

Whatever he wanted to do, Fabius was supported by his parents' money. At first his father wished for a heroic pursuit for his son. He wanted Fabius to have a military career, like the Roman soldiers who defied death and triumphed, conquered lands and brought back booty for the homeland--treasure, slaves, glory. But Fabius never seemed to share his father's passion, and his mother--though she enjoyed the blood-sport of the gladiators--vehemently opposed her son's being a soldier, a career which would surely eventually mean mutilation and untimely death. And so the father relinquished that dream, along with all the others.

For Fabius was determined to be an actor. He admired people with similar ambitions, and eventually devoted his entire time to this art which his father enjoyed as leisure but could not understand as a life's devotion. As he blossomed into his manhood, Fabius wanted to move from his parents' home into a little rooming-house on Stabian Street near the theater district, a house owned by his father and occupied by actors and other theater people. His parents, frustrated and confused by the difference between their son and themselves, let him go. At a financial loss, his father noted. He had been about to sell the building, because theater artists were notoriously reticent in paying their rent, and who else would want to live there?

Fabius began to see Valeria-Julia less and less, and his conversation, when he did see her, was peppered with references to plays and stagecraft, which were beyond her ability even to imagine, and to women who pursued him. Increasingly he included crude and detailed reminiscences of his sexual encounters. He held the image of other women between them, as if to warn her not to come too close.

Feeling her childhood dream fading, Valeria-Julia clung more desperately. She hated him for not being what she wanted him to be; yet she still loved him for the image that she herself had created. She thought she was an ugly girl with no family or future, with a scar on her forehead to remind her--and him--of her violent past. How could she expect someone like him to love her?

***

Now, as she crouched among the ancient dead on this fateful morning, the memory of their most recent meeting returned with terrifying vividness.

She had not seen him in weeks and was frantic at the thought that she had lost him. Then one evening as she and Tertius were closing the bakery and cleaning up the remnants of the day, suddenly there he was. He was flushed (from the sun or from wine or from both) and his talk was a little loud and a little fast, but she was overjoyed to see him after so many days. The sound of his voice, even before she saw him, excited her, and the sight of his beauty and then the casual touch of his hand brushing against hers made her catch her breath.

"Hey, Valeria-Julia, I've got something to tell you! Good news!"

She didn't care what the news was. She felt a rush of warm happiness that he had come to her.

"What? What?" she asked, hanging up her cloth.

"Come walk with me. Are you about finished here?"

She glanced at Tertius. She and Tertius had been having a fairly lively conversation, but now he had turned a bit surly. Still, he nodded at her. "Go ahead. I'll stack up these pans and that's about all we have to do."

Out on the street, Fabius took her hand and they pranced along swinging arms as they used to do when they were children. "I got a part, a really good part in a fabulous play!" He could hardly contain his triumph. "A new play by Plateaus. He's going to be here, going to come to some of the rehearsals. Some other guys tried out for the part, but I got it!"

She squeezed his hand and laughed aloud. They stopped at a tavern, where they bought a flask of wine. Then, without planning, they found themselves wandering to the mountainside. Their feet naturally took the familiar paths they had trod as children and as youths wandering into maturity. They sank down on the fragrant grass and sipped wine and talked, then became less than coherent, then became silent. The sweet scent of the night air, the chirp of crickets, and as he eased her gently onto the soft carpet of grass, the stars, large and golden, soothed her and excited her more than the wine.

They kissed passionately as in the old days. His hands crept beneath her tunic tenderly caressed her breasts, and moved down, stroking her, and soon they lay naked under the stars and the shadows. He teased her and tantalized her with gentle fingers and eager mouth until her moans became cries, and then he entered her and their passion made the trees sing.

When they finally lay exhausted, still tenderly entwined, she felt a deep sense of peace and joy. She knew that at last he loved her.

She had not seen him since then. Until last night. Last night.

Horrified, she began to run again, up the silent mountain.

THE DAY THE GODS WEPT

Around and around in endless circles, grinding corn for the kind master. But for some reason the mule was not compliant now. He kept bucking and stopping suddenly, as if rebelling against his bondage, jerking Tertius off balance. Tertius cursed and started again, pulling the rebellious mule in the direction they were commanded to go. Not that he, Tertius, wanted to go in that direction himself, but it was, at the moment, expedient.

Something about today defied definition. The burning air was still, and despite the bustle of early morning, there was, beneath it all, a strange silence. There was no shade to protect him from the merciless sun beating down upon him. Sweat covered his arms and legs. Sweat made his hands slippery as he led the mule; sweat ran down his face and stung his eyes. His tunic felt like a heavy blanket. The slave belt was a leaden weight. Something was wrong with today. He felt vaguely troubled.

The mountain rumbled. And nobody noticed. They were used to it.

Trudging around and around the mill, Tertius found that in spite of his discomfort, he kept remembering things better forgotten, exhuming hopes better left buried.

Clara. How old had they been then? Hardly out of their teens. She was tiny, more like a child than a grown woman. Or almost-woman. She was milking a cow in the meadow the first time he saw her--but that glimpse had burned into his heart, solidified into a picture as tangible as a mosaic. She was so small, seated beside the great cow, yet the two were in perfect synchrony. She sat comfortably on a low stool, leaning forward a little, her loose skirt pulled up above her knees, her knees spread, her dark hair falling in a heavy braid down her back, stray strands tumbling around her neck and forehead and cheeks. Tertius paused, walked slower, then stopped and watched her. There was an air of serenity about the scene, which somehow soothed his troubled spirit. The cow stood quietly, except for an occasional flick of her tail and a low moo. Tertius found himself fascinated by the girl's hands, expertly massaging the distended udders, squeezing and stroking as the warm milk gushed out and the udder lay flaccid, relaxed, peaceful.

Tertius had been going into the field to gather droppings for the farm workers to lay on the vegetable fields. New on this farm, he was recovering from a severe beating and was yet unable to do the heavy farm work for which he had been purchased. On his second day there he had hidden crouched under a load of tomatoes in a wagon headed for Naples, but he had been caught and returned to his kind master for constructive discipline. Now, his body aching and his soul seething, he found a little comfort in watching this slave girl gently, gently milking. He watched her for a few seconds. Then she looked up, startled to see someone watching her. He smiled so that she wouldn't be afraid, then backed away and went elsewhere to collect droppings.

He encountered her many times after that. Her name was Clara, he learned, and she was a kitchen helper, but often she was made to do other work on the farm, in the field, or in the house. There was no rest for her ever. Small as she was, she did heavy work and carried heavy burdens, Yet her face in repose, as when she milked the cow, was serene, as if her real self lived in some peaceful place beyond the realities of slavery.

They became friends. They became lovers. Tertius both loved and hated her serenity; she seemed to acquiesce without bitterness to the degradation of slavery. He needed her serenity to calm his tortured spirit, but he also wanted her to share his rage. Still, the fire and ice within him began to moderate in the warmth of her love. He began to learn again how to give and how to accept. On some level of himself, he began to realize, without codifying the thought into words, that the benchmark of love is not so much one's impact on the other person as the changes in oneself, the growth toward one's own infinite possibilities. The scars of slavery remained, but under her work-roughened hands, the scars softened. Yet as their love deepened, so did his resentment of his powerlessness. He had nothing to offer her. No plans. No future. Nothing.

They had a kind master. He let them live together in a hut that overlooked green fields. Clara, younger than Tertius and never badly mistreated, blossomed. She was like a dry stick which, thrust into fertile earth, magically sprouts roots and branches and leaves, a dry stick which miraculously flowers and fruits.

Tertius' progress toward transformation was more gradual and less evident but just as real. Open wounds in his spirit began slowly to heal. But he chafed more than ever at his chains. For now he had more at stake. He thought now in terms of manumission rather than escape. Some slaves were freed, he knew that, and some even became successful and highly respected citizens. Those manumissions seemed to occur more frequently in urban areas, Tertius thought, rather than in remote areas such as theirs, but they had a kind master: he would surely listen to Tertius' plea. Still, something in Tertius was uneasy.

Their nights together in the old hut were the life-giving force that sustained them through the toil of their days.

In autumn Clara's beauty reached its zenith. Her hair thickened and grew long and glossy, so that she had to pin it up during the day, but at night Lucius loosened it, and when they loved, it flowed upon him like a soft stream. Her skin became rosy as a ripe peach under the gentle sun. She glowed with a quiet joy. Or perhaps it was Lucius' growing love and happiness (or now, years later, the enchantment of memory) that made her seem so wondrously beautiful. Or perhaps what he sensed then--and now-- was the radiance which suffuses every woman pregnant with a wanted child.

The anticipation of a child brought Tertius both joy and despair. For a slave to create another slave, for a slave to love and cherish a woman and thus to create a child to be a slave, for a slave to bring into the world another like himself, for a slave to create a child whose destiny he could not guide--that was something unnatural. Fearful. Yet some deeper part of himself felt a new joy. Until Clara, he had dealt with slavery with rage and rebellion and flight. He still felt the rage, but now he would have to follow through with his plan for manumission. He tamed his ever-present rage through physical labor and through the softness of Clara's love. He began to have a little faith in the future.

At first the pregnancy went well. Working in the kitchen, Clara ate heartily and flourished. But as the months wore on, the work itself never diminished. There was no time for rest; there was no relief from toil. Never strong, she began to wilt. By the fifth month, when she began to feel the child moving inside, her complexion had sallowed, her hair hung limp, her glow vanished like the flame of a flickering candle. Tertius watched the transformation with growing alarm. His fear intensified with his frustration, and all that he could do was to cradle her in his arms at night. In the seventh month the child was born prematurely, a tiny girl whose head was no bigger than a shriveled apple, whose cry was so weak it could hardly be heard. She was little more than a skeleton covered with transparent skin red with the blood flowing sullenly beneath it. Clara tried to suckle her, but the child was too weak to suck. The baby's death was hardly even a death, because she had scarcely been alive. It was more like a fading away, a quiet evening slipping into night.

In the days that followed, Clara was inconsolable. Passionate weeping gave way to hours of silence and empty staring into nothingness. Warm milk dribbled from her swollen breasts, spilling uselessly onto her distended stomach. Her nipples were hard and tender and useless. When he returned from the fields, Tertius urged her to eat and tried to feed her as one would feed a little child, then not knowing what else to do, held her and stroked her wild hair until she drifted into a troubled sleep. Then he went outside their hut and paced, trying in vain to contain his grief and frustration and rage.

Now, trudging in futile circles behind the mule, Tertius struggled to suppress the intrusive memory. Deliberately he had not thought of Clara for years. But in spite of himself he had to recall the ultimate agony, which had made him the shell that he was today. For the master, of course, had heard about Clara's pregnancy and loss. By whatever cruel coincidence that the gods had concocted--if indeed there were gods at all--the master's daughter, living in Napoli had given birth three months previously. Her baby boy was not thriving, and she was seeking a slave woman to be a wet nurse. When Lucius came back from the fields one day, Clara was gone. Other slaves told him what had happened. Even now, he could not remember the next days and weeks.

Clara returned once or twice for a few hours when the master's daughter brought her baby to visit, but Clara was different. She had gained weight and seemed well-cared-for. But she rebuffed Tertius' joyful caresses and told him that she had promised not to make love to him for a year, because if she became pregnant her milk would dry up. She was remote. She was a stranger. She was broken.

After a few months she did not return. He resumed his old cycle of rebellion, escaping, being brought back and beaten, and finally being sold. The years passed.

He never saw Clara again. He became what he now was. He walked behind the mule, grinding grain for the kind master.

***

"Valeria--Valeria-Julia--Are you here? Where are you?--Valeria--"

Startled, Lucius and Statia froze for a second, then rushed outside. They stared, unbelieving, at the apparition limping toward them. Behind it, they glimpsed Petronia stumbling frantically up the stairs to the rooms, calling out something that was lost in a gust of hot summer wind.

"Who--What's the---" Lucius hung his mouth open, speechless.

People who had started to gather in the courtyard paused to see what was going on. At first nobody was certain that the apparition was only Marcella. Her voice was loud and high- pitched, almost a scream. Her black garment, donned in haste, hung loose about her spare body. Her arms flailed as if, in her blindness, she was seeking something solid to hold onto. Her stick, clutched in one hand, seemed to fly with life of its own. Her long white hair was disheveled, falling about her shoulders and over her contorted face.

"Where is she? Where's my girl? Valeria-Julia!"

Lucius' first coherent thought was, "She's really crazy! She's lost her mind!" What was he to do with her? And where indeed was Valeria-Julia? Had this crazy woman killed her? He looked anxiously toward the steps to their rooms, Petronia was groping her way down the steps-- alone.

Now Marcella was struggling visibly for control, grappling with panic. "Is she here? Where is she?" Marcella had by now reached the counter. She leaned heavily against the counter and stabbed the air with her stick. "Where?"

"She's not here, Marcella," Statia gasped. "We thought she was upstairs with you, sick or something." Marcella groaned. "Come here, sit down," said Statia softly. "You're all upset. Come on in here---"

"NO!" Lucius shouted, taking a cautious step toward Marcella. He was not an inhumane man, but he was a man of business, and to have a madwoman in his bakery would scare the customers away. "Statia, take her back upstairs. Marcella, go on upstairs now. Valeria-Julia is all right. She'll be back soon. Go on upstairs with...."

"NO!" Marcella was leaning on her staff now, looking into chaos with sightless eyes. "This is the day of the prophesy! Run---all of you---get out---the day of the prophesy!" By now she had turned and was hobbling blindly toward the street, sweeping her cane in front of her. "The prophesy!" Her voice seemed to echo and reverberate.

Lucius and the women stared after her, speechless. Tertius was struggling toward the cubicle, a large sack of cornmeal on his shoulder and a lesser one under his arm. He glimpsed the others staring into the courtyard, mouths open. His own cry broke the trance. "What's the matter? What's wrong? Who was here?"

"Marcella's gone crazy,"Petronia gasped. "She was here looking for Valeria-Julia."

"Valeria-Julia's not here yet?" Tertius had a sudden stab of foreboding. He cursed himself now because he had not gone to see about her before. Where was she?

Lucius was pacing the floor, not sure what to do. Statia spoke up in wonder, not talking especially to Tertius, "Marcella's talking about this is the day of some prophecy. What's she talking about?"

"Nothing--nothing--" shouted Lucius. "Just get on back to work. Tertius, did you put the mule into the stable? Take the meal into the---"

But Tertius was gone. Dropping the bags of cornmeal, he dashed up the outside stairs into the room above. A quick look around the sparse room showed a palpable and resounding emptiness. "Valeria-Julia!" he roared into the silence. He dashed back downstairs and into the street. Vaguely he heard Lucius yelling, "TERTIUS! GET BACK HERE! TERTIUS!!"

Tertius still wore the slave belt. But from this moment he was free.

The mountain rumbled softly. The earth trembled. But nobody noticed.

THE DAY THE GODS WEPT

VI

Tertius had not heard his master's angry cries calling him back into slavery. He fled from the cul-de-sac, away from oven, oxen, and bakery.

He rushed through the streets, crowded now with shoppers, merchants, workers of various kinds, his eyes desperately searching for the humped, black-clad form. Now and then he would ask a shopkeeper or someone he recognized from the bakery, "Have you seen old Marcella? Has she been past here?" Usually the answer was no, but finally the answer was, "Yes, she was here a while ago. She's gone crazy, man. Stopping people and yelling about that prophesy of hers. I would've tried to take her home, but I couldn't leave the shop." Someone else said, "Yeah, she was running down the street--well, as close as she could come to running, telling people to get away because this was the day of some prophesy. Waving that cane like some kind of weapon. Calling for that girl Valeria-Julia. She stumbled on this curb, and we had to pick her up."Someone else added, "Looked like she was lost. Nobody really paid her any mind except a bunch of kids running behind her laughing. Little bastards! She headed down Stabia Street. Did Lucius send you after her?"

But Tertius was rushing toward Stabia Street. The house of the actors! She was trying to get to the house of the actors, where Fabius lived. The Temple of Isis

71

was down that way. Maybe that's where she was going. He had to find her, to help her and to find out what she knew about Valeria-Julia. The prophesy! He was one of the few who had believed the prophesy.

He had seen her on that day, on the steps of the temple. He was new in the city then; Lucius had just recently bought him, and he was a little lost in the city. He was on an errand to the fish market and, seeing several people staring at the temple steps, he stopped. The image of Marcella had clung to him and recurred to him now, as he frantically searched. On that day so many years ago she had sat on the temple steps, her thin white garment flowing around her spare body like sea water around a rock. She was gripping a fancy carved staff, leaning into it a little, as if it were a source not of physical support but of wisdom, a link with the gods. It seemed to him that the carved snakes writhed, rustling the carved vines. Yet she sat absolutely still; only the white hair around her face moved, rumpled by the early autumn breeze. Her eyes were closed, as if she looked inward. Her swarthy face was the embodiment of peace--the profound peace that follows agony. Then she began to speak.

***

Augusta enjoyed strolling through the streets of Pompeii. By now the shops and booths were open, and the air was filled with the hubbub of buying and selling, bargaining and haggling. A little band of street musicians were playing cymbals and a flute while a portly middle-aged man did a clown-dance with surprising grace. An elderly shop- keeper dozed in a chair beside his fruit stand, and two giggling little boys snitched an apple and an orange. A stately woman, accompanied by her servant, strolled from one shop to another, her long dress flowing about her legs and ankles. The servant staggered under the increasingly heavy burden of packages. An aging prostitute chatted with two sailors from the ship that lay anchored in the harbor. Two or three elderly men sat at a table outside a little outdoor cafe munching on sausage or fried fish, sipping watered wine, and arguing politics. An adolescent boy dashed down the street with a little dog yapping merrily at his heels. Carts rattled on the cobblestones, almost drowning out the clip-clop of the horses' hooves. There was the usual bustle, a sense of life reaching out to life, as if life would last forever.

If the earth trembled a little, if the mountain rumbled softly, nobody heeded except perhaps an ancient man or woman who might glance earthward or skyward and, finding no answer to a half-formed question, sink again into torpor.

**

In Lucius' bakery there was the usual ebb and flow of customers. Understaffed now, Lucius, together with Statia, served the customers while Petronia tended the oven. Usually this was the part of his business that Lucius enjoyed most--chatting with people, listening to their conversations and occasionally joining in, being called upon to mediate differences of opinion, laughing with them at jokes and funny stories, asking about the outcomes of their dilemmas. Estella had been the manager and money-counter. But for him the artistry of baking and the mingling with people had been the life-blood of his living.

Today, though, was different. It was intensely hot, and he had not had a chance to eat. His physical discomfort, however, was exceeded by a sense of foreboding. Where was Valeria-Julia? What had happened to her? What was wrong with old Marcella? Was she suffering from the inevitable ravages of age, or was this something different? And he would have to devise some kind of punishment for Tertius. And something--something indefinable--was awry.

The beekeeper came, bringing honey. Lucius could never think of his name; he was young and new to the business, the old beekeeper having died on his mountain farm some months ago. In answer to Lucius' polite inquiry, the young beekeeper responded, "Oh, the family's fine. The bees aren't producing as much as I thought, though. They're pretty active, but they seem sort of--well--agitated or something. Well, I guess they'll settle down. I'll see you next time."

Customers came and went, most of them comfortably familiar. Lucius found some relief from his own anxieties through listening to wisps of their conversations.

"Two heads!" a woman was saying to her buddies, continuing their conversation. "I never heard of such a thing. Two heads!"

"That's what he said," replied the other woman. "Scared him too bad to do anything at all until the thing had slithered across the path into the brush on the other side, with that one tail a- whipping. By the time he got himself together and went looking for it, it was gone."

"But a snake with two heads!" exclaimed another woman.

"Well, he thought at first to kill it. But he couldn't find it by then." The women were turning away from the counter, having concluded their business with Lucius. "He came back to the house to get a net or something to catch it in. He thought to throw it into the flames at the Vulcan festival last night. But when he got back to the path, it was gone."

The first woman laughed loudly, and as they left, Lucius barely heard her say, "Are you sure he wasn't into that wine that he makes...?" The women left, laughing.

A little slave girl approached the counter, bearing her mistress' baby on her hip. They came every Wednesday, this strange little pair. Usually it was Valeria-Julia who waited on them, but today they had to come to Lucius. He had seen them many times, of course, but today he was, for some reason, moved by them--by the contrast, perhaps. The slave child-- somewhere around fourteen, he guessed, though maybe older and stunted (certainly her eyes were old)--was thin, her legs mildly bowed, her cheeks slightly sunken, her hair thin and wispy. The slave belt hung loose around her waist. The baby she held, a toddler, was fat and rosy, his dark curls clinging to his damp neck and forehead. Yet the baby, usually so ebullient, was quiet now clutching the girl around the neck and sucking his thumb, his head on the girl's shoulder. The slave girl held the baby tenderly, in spite of the heat and the weight of her burden.

"Two loaves, please," the slave-girl said softly, placing her copper coins on the counter.

Lucius spoke to her kindly. "Here are some just cooled from the oven." The round loaves, each shaped into eight rosettes, were golden brown, soft, and deliciously aromatic. He slipped the loaves into her basket.

The little girl turned to leave. Lucius felt oddly compelled to say something more to her.

"What is your name, little one?"

She turned and smiled a tiny smile. He saw that her teeth were yellow and pitted.

"Grace," she said as she trudged away. "Grace."

Three men were standing at the corner of the counter, deep in an intense discussion. Sooner or later they would buy bread or perhaps some cakes, but their main purpose seemed to be to continue their perpetual debate. One of the men was Abraham, a Jew; a second was a man named Marcus, who belonged to this new religion out of Jerusalem; the third, whose name Lucius didn't know, seemed to have no particular point of view but darted in and out of the conversation, injecting a question here and a buzz-word there to set the others off and intensify the argument. Nobody was ever convinced one way or the other; nobody changed or even modified his opinion. The discussion had been going on for months and appeared to have no prospect of ending.

"I tell you, the world is corrupt and evil, and God will destroy it," Marcus was saying.

"How come you people are so gloomy?" Abraham responded. "Just look around. It's a good world. Look at Pompeii. Not perfect, but look at all we have...."

"Yes, look!" Marcus' hand waved in a wide arc, sweeping over the whole scene. "Worldliness! Look at those people prancing around in their fancy clothes, spending money like water. Fancy clothes, big houses. They're not thinking about the afterlife-- they're too busy good-timing and sinning and fornicating!" His gesturing hand was pointing now to a bit of graffiti on a nearby wall, praising a commercial woman's charms.

"Yeah, but didn't I used to see you..." began the third man.

"That was before I was converted!" roared Marcus. The other men chuckled, and Marcus fumed.

"I still say Pompeii is blessed," said Abraham finally, trying to get the argument back on track. "If it wasn't blessed, why would all those rich people come here to build their mansions and grow old and fat here? "

"Money!" hooted Marcus. "Things of the world. Money doesn't mean that anybody is smart or even good. It just means that you can buy things."

"Well, what about the philosophers and poets and scholars and people like that? Look here, man..." He began to intone names: "Cicero, Seneca, Pliny...You start adding them up. Why, those ships down at the harbor, they're always bringing in some sage from Greece or..."

Marcus shouted, "Yes, and those same ships bring in slaves!"

"The slaves are a big part of our wealth! I still say Pompeii is blessed."

The third man spoke up. "Who is it that sends us these 'blessings'?

"God, who loves us," Abraham responded immediately.

"Satan, who tempts us," cried Marcus. "I've studied scripture, man. God destroyed the world once because of sin, and He'll destroy it again. Last time God destroyed the world by floods. Next time--fire."

Lucius turned away. He was sick of this futile, unproductive talk. He was hot and he was hungry. And he was disturbed. It was getting on toward mid-day. Soon the morning rush would wane, and whether or not Tertius and Valeria-Julia were back, he would take his usual midday break--lunch with a cool drink of wine and water, some good conversation with his cronies, then a leisurely half hour or so at the bath house. Three baths--first hot for cleansing, then tepid for relaxation, then cool for invigoration. The afternoon would be better.

A well-dressed man had sauntered up to the counter, a stranger. Obviously he was a man of some importance; he wore an off-white toga with a purple border. Lucius went to wait on him. Ordinarily Lucius would have been delighted with this man's patronage. Today, however, had already brought too many distractions, and Lucius had deliberatively turned his thoughts from today's troubles to Augusta and the child they were expecting. He would have to get her a slave to take care of the baby--one who could suckle the child if he was lucky enough to find one who had recently given birth, or if not, at least a young girl to do the demanding work of child care. Something about the slave girl Grace and the baby who clung to her lingered in his thoughts. He treated his slaves better than Grace had obviously been treated. (He felt a surge of anger at that ungrateful Tertius.) Turning his attention to his customer's order and the immediate task of getting through the day, he still could not rid himself of the image of those two faces, the slave girl's and the wealthy baby's, and the two pairs of sad eyes, whose incomprehensible sadness linked them together.

The customer left, and a beggar came pleading for bread. The debate between Marcus and Abraham was winding down, still unresolved; they would soon come to the counter and buy their bread. Lucius glanced toward the sky, toward Vesuvius. The unremitting sun was almost overhead. Almost noon. Time for a break.

***

Valeria-Julia trudged wearily, one heavy leg dragging the other. She had walked for so long. The hard ground was no longer level but jagged, slanting upward. Her breath came in harsh rasps. She had left the rutted dirt road where farmers drove their carts to and from town. She was enclosed in her misery. The rattle of the wagons and the cheery greetings of the farmers intruded upon her aloneness. She picked her way up the mountainside, pulling herself up by the tough dry grass ahead. Her thighs ached; her legs trembled. Her arms and legs were peppered with insect bites, stinging and itching. Her hands were not bloody now, for she had long since wiped her sweaty palms on her tunic. Now and then she rested on a rock, fanning away the noisome gnats and mosquitoes. The air was thick and hard to breathe. The sun was directly overhead, blazing angrily down upon her, burning her like the wrath of retribution.

She was lost. She wandered aimlessly, her sense of any destination gone. Having left the road, she was in a realm of wild growth and rocks and ruts, dry ground and crawling things. The mountain which had been her refuge was now alien. Hostile. No hiding place.

She sought the foot-path which she and Fabius, children with all of this ahead, used to follow to the copse of trees that formed their play-home. But now the path was overgrown with weeds, and she could not find it. She stared around wildly. Nothing looked familiar. Where was the road? She needed desperately to get back to the road. She cried out once in panic, but there was no one to hear. There were no strayed cattle, not even any buzzards circling overhead, seeking to feed on the dead. Silence blanketed her world. She stumbled from one futile direction to another, but still there was nothing to tell her where she was or how to get back to familiar ground. She stepped into a ditch, fell, lay for a moment dizzy and confused, then struggled to her feet. A deep pain gripped her left ankle, and once again she cried out. She sank down on the unwelcoming earth, folding her legs. She was trying to make herself as small as possible, wishing that she could disappear from the hostile world. She clasped her hands around her legs and pressed her forehead against her knees. She moaned once--a keening, really, rather than a moan. For now she remembered. She and Fabius. Fabius. Something deep within her had thought that if she could find the place of their childhood, the years would be erased--they would be children again. Fabius would live again. To erase the years and begin again!

If only time could be snatched back, if only life could be re-lived!

She closed her eyes and began to sink into a strange torpor. Fragments of the old nightmare returned. Fragments of near-memory before memory. Once again she clung to the other baby, the other self. The one she had always followed, whose cries had always brought the mother scurrying with food or dry clothes or comfort. The half of herself who grabbed bread from her hands and pushed her down but who cried in sympathy when she cried and whose chubby arm or leg was flung protectively over her as they slept, two halves of the same whole.

Marcella had told her--but she knew only in nightmares--that the mother and the twin toddlers were asleep in the low wooden bed when the earthquake came. In nightmares she--the baby who later became Valeria-Julia--was jerked awake by the heaving of the bed, the violent shaking when her insides seemed to separate bone from bone, and a terrible roar reverberated in her ears. Then there was a deafening crash and the earth shook and her world collapsed around her. Marcella later told her that an oil lamp had apparently fallen from a table, and the wooden floor had caught fire. In nightmares the red-yellow flames surrounded the bed, rushed toward them, all around them, burning them, flames hissing like snakes and licking out at them like the tongues of snakes. Shrieks as her mother threw herself on top of the babies, legs kicking and arms flailing, Then a desperate clinging to the other baby, then a sharp pain as something hit her forehead. Then waking as the other baby, now limp and silent and slippery, was wrenched from her grasp.

Valeria-Julia would awaken from the nightmare gasping for breath, too terrified to scream. In her little-girl years she would cling to Marcella, who would hold her close and soothe her back to a different reality. But even as she grew up, the nightmare was always there, lurking inside her, ready to strike. As time passed, the nightmare came less frequently, and as she grew, she was learning to deal with it. But it was still there. For the gods--or destiny or chance--having destroyed whatever love she had known, sent her forth on her life's journey with half herself missing, with a fearful chasm which could be neither defined nor filled.

She was forever scarred. She was set forth into her world a beggar for love.

And now, as she crouched lost on the mountainside, the earth trembled again. She threw her head back and clasped her hands to her face and moaned. Fabius. For now she remembered.

She remembered it all.

VII

"Shit!" Lucius muttered to himself. Nothing was going right today. Valeria-Julia was gone, Marcella had lost her mind in his shop, and Tertius--a slave!!-- had defied him and fled. Lucius had an uncomfortable feeling that perhaps he should have sent someone out to look for Valeria-Julia, or even gone himself. She had been a faithful worker; if she wasn't there by now, something bad must have happened. And, he realized in his worry, she was more than just a faithful worker. He had watched her grow up in his shop. He had trained her in the business and felt joy in her quickness and intelligence. And yes, he cared about her. His own tension had mounted during the morning. Well, there was nobody to send now. Statia and Petronia were needed in the bakery. But he felt restless and uncomfortable not knowing where she was or what had happened to her. He would have to do something himself. Shit! But what? Where would he go? Lucius searched his memory for any clue about where she could have gone. He began to realize how little he knew about this girl who had worked with him since she was barely in her teens. She talked seldom, even to Statia and Petronia, and he had no idea what her life was like when she was not working. He thought long and hard as he attended to the morning's business.

Then at some point, selling a rosette of bread, he suddenly remembered: Several times he had seen her talking to a young man--what was his name? Fabius. Lucius knew the boy's family. His father had sold Lucius his house; that's why he remembered the boy. The boy had become some kind of actor. Hadn't he been in some play Lucius had seen in the theater? Yes, he had taken Augusta, and she had cheered so loudly at the end that Lucius had been a little embarrassed. Then a few days later he had noticed Valeria-Julia talking with him in a most familiar manner at the bakery. Her face had been lit with something Lucius had never seen in her before; her plain face had been almost beautiful. Transfixed. A thought had flashed through Lucius' consciousness and faded before he could fully acknowledge it: Would Augusta ever light up like that in *his* presence? Lucius never realized the thought, but the image of Valeria-Julia in love did recur to him now. Fabius--was he possibly at the theater rehearsing for the play that had been announced in the latest graffiti? Or in that house near the theater where it was said that some of the company lived? Well, he would soon take a break--things were winding down at the shop-- and before going to lunch and the baths, he would go down to that part of town and see whether he could find Fabius and ask him whether he had seen Valeria-Julia. Damn! Shit! Where in hell was Tertius? Lucius would have to devise a special punishment for Tertius!

***

Augusta strolled easily over the cobbled streets, her long legs striding along briskly but without hurry. She was later than she had planned--it had taken her forever to get out of the house--but he would just have to wait. The tension of waiting, and even his mild irritation, would increase his desire, and by the time she got there, he would be crazy for her! She smiled a little smugly. She enjoyed strolling the city. All her life, until Lucius, she had seen little but the farm high on the mountain. She had waded barefoot in chicken shit and cow shit and horse shit and mud. Her feet were tough enough to walk on stone and never bleed. Nothing was soft in her life except the mud and shit that oozed between her toes. And, as she grew older, the desire in men's eyes.

Augusta loved the city. She loved the city's hustle and bustle. There were bright murals depicting the heroic events of the past and the affluence of the present, official announcements on billboards, and messages which passers-by scribbled on the walls proclaiming their loves, irritations with neighbors, sexual longings, political preferences, whatever was on their hearts. She loved the sounds of people going about their business in the city. She enjoyed voices greeting one another or quarreling or even singing. Sometimes she caught a bit of coherent conversation. Now, standing at a curb as a mule-driven cart carrying vegetables rumbled by, she heard a man standing behind her, probably a farmer, saying to his companion, "...too dry on the mountain....grass all dried up....goats skinny, starving.....lost two already...." The cart passed and everybody moved. Demurely Augusta crossed Stabia Street on the stepping stones provided for the pedestrians to protect them from sloshing through the slippery mess in the street--garbage, trash of all kinds, and even human waste.

On the other side of the street were a cluster of shops and several restaurants. She loved the shops. They gave the city a sense of movement, a feeling of ongoing life. Stall-owners and shopkeepers sang the wonders of their wares. A wine-merchant waved an ivy branch, and a butcher waved a myrtle branch to show that his meat was fresh from the mountain, where myrtle grew. Colorful signs announced the goodies inside; hawkers offered the passers-by free samples and other temptations. "I've got fresh fish, fresh from the bay," caroled a fish monger. "Fruit from up the mountain," sang another, offering Augusta a slice of pomegranate. A butcher promised delicacies: "Turkey, duck, and fattened mice, already stuffed and roasted!" A colorful sign announced, "Spices from Egypt and Indonesia." Ordinarily Augusta would have stopped and perhaps bought something that would delight her, for Lucius always saw to it that she had money in her purse. The aroma of fried fish or sausage did make her hungry. But for some reason, today she felt compelled to keep moving. Without pausing, she noted that men's eyes followed her, as they always did. She was glad that she hadn't worn the stola, that ugly garment that married women were supposed to wear. Ugh!

Shoppers poured in and out of the shops, crowding the narrow sidewalks. Augusta's arm lightly brushed the arm of a young prostitute going in the other direction. One could usually recognize a prostitute because of the rough tunic she wore; there were several brothels in the area. The woman gave Augusta a quick frown, then resumed her customary smile of invitation and walked on. Augusta recalled her own thoughts of not-too-long-ago: Rather than spend her life on the farm and end up like her mother and sisters, she might have moved to the city and tried her luck as a prostitute. Lucius had come along at just the right time, and look at her now!

Augusta stopped and sipped some sweet water from a public fountain. She was a little irritated that the water pressure was low, and the water was not cool. But it slaked her thirst for the moment. She walked on but had to duck out of the way when a litter borne by slaves brushed by, carrying an elderly man of obvious importance. Two African slaves ran ahead of the litter shouting, "Make way! Make way!" Augusta wondered idly whether she would have been trampled if she hadn't ducked in time.

She passed a pharmacy, a smithy, a few groceries, a shop with ritualistic perfumes and scents to prepare the dead for their final journey, and numerous outdoor cafes. She loved the vibrancy which the shops brought to the city. Things available, desires which could now be satisfied, needs previously unsuspected, now to be met. Dreams which she had never dared to dream on the farm, dreams which would never have occurred to her there--here they were, spread before her, cried out by hawkers as she passed, each a part of the great chorus, a siren song of desires which, once defined, could be satisfied.

She knew, but took no heed today, that beneath the splendor of Pompeii was a dark underside. Beneath the sparkling fountains and the convenience of the toilets, public and private, was a complicated sewer system leading to the sea. And beneath the splendor of the Basilica in the forum just a few blocks from here, with its court system and the unremitting rhetoric of the politicians, was the dungeon, where prisoners were chained to the wall in complete darkness.

Augusta stumbled, caught herself, and avoided falling. Yes, she was almost—but not quite--used to wearing shoes. For another instant her thoughts fled back to the farm. A curious thought followed: Where are the cats? There had been lots of cats on the farm. From little-girlhood she had loved the cats and their myriad kittens. Most of her few gentle memories centered on cats--cuddling their furry little selves, then admiring their independence, their ability to give or withhold their affection as they chose. As she grew older she came to enjoy the way a cat would stretch luxuriously in a little piece of sunshine or purr and groom itself before a fire. She missed her cats when she married Lucius, but she always noticed the numerous cats that snoozed in the doorways of the shops or sauntered through the streets on business of their own. But today she had seen no cats. Where were they? Weird. Well--not worth thinking about. She thrust the idea away as quickly as it came.

She was going to meet her lover. But she felt a strange uneasiness. She was not a thinker. The directions of her life had moved according to visceral feelings. Hens and roosters, cows and bulls, the grunts and groans of her sisters and their lovers in the grass---these had charted the paths for her to follow. Lucius had been a way out of the shit and the mud. She was wearing shoes now and living in a fancy house with servants! and all that she had to do was to let him do what men always did to women and bulls always did to cows. And she could still have a lover who knew what to do to make her cry out and then to leave him with joy, floating above the cobbled streets.

What was wrong with her this morning? What was interfering with her joy?

Was it the new life inside her?

She had not envisioned this inconvenience in her body as a real baby. It was a swelling and tenderness in her breasts, a slight nausea and dizziness when her stomach was empty, an increased hunger for food and a diminished hunger for sex. But a baby!

Her steps slowed. She paused at a little shop which sold fruit and wine. Lucius had walked here with her a few days ago and had, in fact, bought her flowers from a child-peddler outside. A little girl, perhaps a farm child from the mountainside. She had had a flash of memory of the spicy eucalyptus and the sweet-scented alyssum that grew along the roadside when she herself was a child. And a memory of her stern-faced father whose rare moments of gentleness had chained her forever to the hope that he would love her.

Augusta was approaching the Small Theater, empty now, where she and Lucius had enjoyed musical performances and mime. Lucius had introduced her to theater here. She smiled to herself. The people called this the Small Theater, as opposed to the nearby Large Theater, but she, fresh from the country, had been overwhelmed by the arched entrances, the huge semi-circle of seats extending high up to the great roof, the twenty or so tuff steps to the upper levels, the arcade at the bottom, the intimidating statues, the excited crowds--oh, the whole scene! Even now, her breath came short as she remembered that first moment. Later he had taken her to the Large Theatre across the arcade, and she knew that nothing, nothing could equal that wonder. Lucius had reveled in her passion for the plays, the actors, the spectacle. Why, who could believe such a thing! To reorder a world, one's own world, and see it living and breathing, alive! Sometimes when the scene ended, she glanced at Lucius and saw that instead of watching the play, he was watching her. Now, a sudden image of Lucius' proud face flashed across her memory. He loved showing her new things and seeing her grow.

The child-self, barefoot, wearing her sisters' cast-off dress, picking flowers by the roadside--how could that child have grown into the now-Augusta? The answer tumbled out before the question was fully formed: Lucius had created her, the Augusta of now. Out of the dust and dung of the farmyard, Lucius had made her and breathed life into her. Or at least had opened the way for her to become all that she could be.

And now she was dawdling on the way to meet her lover.

**

Trembling on the trembling earth, Valeria-Julia remembered. Yesterday morning she had awakened still unrested, still troubled and angry because Fabius was nowhere to be found. Why had he not come to her? Or was he somewhere sick or hurt, needing her? The heat of the day was already stifling, even at this early hour; she was sweating, and her hair was stuck to her damp neck and forehead. She washed and dressed languidly in the predawn dark, pulling on the loin cloth underwear and the rough tunic, and slipping into the stiff sandals. As she backed down the wooden steps to the bakery, she felt, as she always did, even now in her restlessness, how beautiful the world was at this moment between darkness and light.

Petronia and Statia both arrived at the bakery at the same time as Valeria-Julia. They were carrying lighted candles, which they set on the work-table in the cubicle. Valeria-Julia recalled with a start that today was Vulcanalia--the day of the festival to Vulcan, the god of fire. Many people began the day by the light of candles, a tribute to the blessings which fire had bestowed upon them. Marcella had often told Valeria-Julia, to allay her childhood fears, that fire-- beginning with the sun--had given them life and kept them alive. But to Valeria-Julia the unremembered memory of fire destroying her world, was deep in the crevasses of her being.

"What fire doesn't destroy," Marcella said, "it purifies." But for Valeria-Julia, the fear remained.

"Well, where's your candle?" Statia asked Valeria-Julia.

"Oh, I forgot," Valeria-Julia replied, smiling. She smiled a lot but said little.

"Forgot your candle!" Statia could hardly believe it.

Petronia was already laying out the flour, water. and flavoring for the dough. "We need some more anise," she said to Victoria-Julia. To Statia she said, "Don't worry about the candles."

"Why not? She forgot her candle last year, too, don't you remember?"

They got on with their routine work. Because it was Vulcanalia, they were surrounded by candles burning, burning. Flames dancing when the breeze from outside caught them or flames reaching upward when there was no wind. Because Vulcan was also the god of trades related to ovens, including theirs, bakers were particularly intense in their obeisance to Vulcan.

"Is your mother going to hang your cloth things out in the sun?" Statia asked Petronia as they began their kneading.

Petronia laughed. "What we've got, yes. I hope Vulcan'll be satisfied with that." They both laughed. "Are you going to the bonfire after work?" she asked Statia.

"Sure. Wouldn't miss it for anything."

Valeria-Julia, looking for another jar of anise, had her back to them. She shuddered. She thought of that terrible bonfire that Marcella had taken her to, years ago when she was still a little girl. She had clung to Marcella's skirt, terrified by the fire and fascinated by the flames. But when she heard the screams, she screamed, too, in wild hysteria. For the screams were coming from little animals which were being flung alive into the fire, each one a sacrifice to Vulcan. Fish, puppies, kittens, snakes, even lambs. Screaming. And as she remembered it, even the fish, mouths gaping, screamed, and even the snakes, wriggling and twisting, hissed so loudly that the hisses became screams. And she, a little girl scarred, she screamed, too, as the little creatures were flung into the fire.

When Lucius closed the bakery yesterday evening, Valeria-Julia surrendered to the depression and smoldering anger that had hung dark and heavy above her days. She had not seen Fabius since the night when, warmed by wine, he had loved her so passionately on the mountain. The softness of the grass and the firmness of the earth beneath her, the weight of his body, the scent of him and the sound of his sighs, his fragmented words, his climactic cry had come to her vaguely in dreams and clung to her days like mist.

After the loving, he had not sought her out, nor had she encountered him by chance, even though her eyes had searched the hordes in the street outside the bakery. Now she had taken to roaming the streets herself after work, down to the marketplace, the Forum, even as far as the seaside, gazing into the little groups of youths who laughed together and exchanged loud confidences in the streets and outdoor cafes, mingling in crowds, roaming quiet residential areas. Hoping to glimpse him, hoping to see the sparkle in his eyes when he encountered her, when she knew that in spite of everything, he did love her. But as day after day and night after night of futile searching ended in bitter frustration, dimming hope was replaced by rising anger that was now a crescendo of rage.

Sometimes she lingered around the house of the actors, but even late into the night, he never returned. She went home to the barren rooms which she and Marcella shared, and she tossed sleepless to another dawn. Marcella's sonorous snoring, comforting in her childhood, a reminder of the solid reality of love and care, was little more to her now than background music for her pain. She had disturbing dreams these nights, incoherent fragments of memory, in which everything she loved was swept away from her, and love itself forever vanished. And she clung to the dead remnants of love as she had clung all that night to her dead twin.

What did she know now of love except what her ripening body taught her? So she roamed the streets seeking Fabius. Seeking love.

As the days passed, she became more agitated rather than less so. She worked as usual in the bakery, and nobody noticed that she was even quieter than always. The heat these days was oppressive, but then heat always was intense in August.

And suddenly yesterday evening, there he was, on the sidewalk in front of a brothel. He was surrounded by a gaggle of young men laughing raucously and gulping from flagons of wine. Two women hovered near him; the laughter seemed to focus on the women, and one of them leaned familiarly on Fabius's shoulder. His face was ruddy with suntan and wine. His hair was burnished gold like the sunset. Desire and rage battled within Valeria-Julia, and she stood there not knowing whether to berate or to embrace him, or whether she should simply slink away like a whipped dog.

Before she could decide, he saw her. "Hey-- Valeria-Julia!" He made his way to her, grinning happily. At his touch, her rage melted.

They agreed to meet at his room in the actors' house later, after he had finished up some business or other. He rejoined his friends and they disappeared around a nearby corner. Valeria-Julia stood uncertainly, not knowing what to do with herself.

As darkness descended, she trudged down Stabia Street. The crowds had diminished now, the shoppers had gone home with their purchases, and some of the shops were closing. In the sunset, the street began to feel ominous, shadowy now where the sun had once shone. Valeria-Julia walked a little faster. The actors' house was part of a series of rooms and facilities ringing the court in front of the two theaters. There were no shows at the theaters tonight, no sense of frantic activity, no pleasure-seeking crowds. Encased in her inner tumult, Valeria-Julia hardly noticed her surroundings. But the sunset was so glorious that she did glance skyward and for an instant was caught in its beauty. Then it was dark, and she entered the court. In the shadows the rows of rooms were foreboding.

She crouched in front of Fabius' quarters and waited in the purple night. It seemed as if the two warring sides of her self battled, and she did not know how she would greet him. But as he came sauntering toward her, smiling happily, his gait a little unsteady, she melted again, and although part of her seethed inside, she followed him meekly into his sparsely-furnished little room. She was a little timid. She had never been in his room before.

The bed was in the center of the room, the first thing one saw—a narrow little bed covered with a rich white blanket inviting rest—or passion. Against the wall was a little table on which was a crystal vase with a wilted single bud.

Fabius was carrying a lighted candle; he had several unlighted candles in his bag. "Hey, sweetheart, look what I've got!" Joyfully he pulled out other candle-holders from various places in the room, stuck the candles in them, and lit the candles. He chatted happily the whole time; he knew that women loved the romance of candlelight. Placed in strategic places, the candles lit up the stark, drab room until it looked like a royal boudoir: shadows dancing, dark corners hiding what should be hidden, light shining, glimmering, bringing joy. The whole room was alight with fire.

Valeria-Julia watched in horror.

***

Here on the mountain, vainly seeking solace in the mountain's indifferent bosom, she remembered with perfect clarity that strange night. He was already half drunk, and she was vacillating between hate and desperate love, the desire to hurt and the desire to heal. Her own conflict fanned her rage, and the rage prevailed. But behind her angry words was a pleading for love, a terrible need for this boy of nineteen to replace all that had been torn from her in her infancy. How could he--how, indeed, could she--have known that?

Unaware of the anger and desire that warred inside her, he turned his back and went to the little table against the wall, where he had set out an amphora of wine, two stemmed glasses, and several pieces of silverware, including a fancy dagger, its handle studded with gemstones.

He handed her a glass of wine, and she took a sip. Her fingers nervously caressed the stem, sliding up and down, up and down the shaft.

She took another sip. He sat her down on the side of the bed, but at his touch her anger spilled over, and she began to berate him for neglecting her. He smiled vaguely, letting her talk, clutching the stem of his glass and taking an occasional gulp. Clutching the stem. Vaguely smiling.

Her jealousy mounted. Her voice became hoarse and raspy, like someone else's voice and not her own. "Yes, you know just how to treat a woman. What am I to you, just another of your women?" The word hung between them, vulgar and accusing. The word stabbed the air.

He answered as if to fill the hole which the word had torn. "Look, baby," he said at last, pouring another glass of wine for each of them, "of course I care for you. You-- you're my little sweety. My first friend, my friend all this time." His words were a little slurred. "But I really can't have a one-on-one relationship with anybody right now. I know too many people, too many women, and there are too many demands on my time. I can't settle down on any one woman. You understand that, don't you?"

They were sitting on the hard bed softened by a soft white blanket. His hand was unsteady. He spilled a little of the red wine on the blanket.

She sipped before she answered. She tried to stop the angry tears. She felt as if he had slapped her.

"Don't cry, honey. Come here." He pulled her to him. Gently he ran his fingers through her hair, pushing it back from her forehead and exposing the livid scar. He did not notice the scar, he was so accustomed to it. But she felt that an ugliness in herself was exposed. He kissed her cheek, and his fingers slid into the neck of her garment and wandered to her breast. His touch was smooth and practiced in spite of his drunkenness, and she had a fleeting thought that she could have been any woman, not particularly herself. She stiffened. But something in her wanted to yield. In spite of herself, her nipple hardened to his touch, and deep inside, her most secret parts became swollen and warm and wet. She desperately wanted to believe that if she loved him hard enough, passionately enough, he would understand her need and would love her. They flung off their clothes and the candlelight flickered on their nude bodies. She let him lay her down on the soft blanket. The sweet wine and her body's demands overwhelmed her sense.

And the lovemaking began. The groping and the grasping, the incoherent muttering, the awful intensity, rising, rising--and as her passion accelerated, so did her anger.

Clasping her arms about him, her breasts crushed against his chest, clasping her legs around him, ready for him to enter her, crying out for him to enter, she was suddenly aware that he was not simply prolonging the passion: He had fallen silent, his arms dangling loosely. His breathing was deep and slow. His body was dead weight, pinning her down to the blanketed bed. Her passion, hot and demanding, had no place to go. It stagnated around her spirit like tepid water.

She cried out in rage and frustration, but his response was only a bubbly sigh. Strengthened by rage, she pushed him aside and wriggled out from under him. For a moment she stood over him cursing and snarling like a wild dog. For she knew now that he would never love her. The center of her life, the fragile hope that had shaped her days, a hope fed by her own need, had been whipped away. Who was she now?

The candles flickered, cast weirding undulating shadows.

She slipped into a dreamlike state, a sense of unreality, as if this were not really happening. She could make out the dim outline of his white body. He lay on his stomach. His face was turned away from her, and she could not see.

Sobbing and trembling and still cursing, she struggled into her clothes, intending to flee from the room, away from her dead hopes. But she could not leave. Something held her there, for she knew on some level of herself that once she left that room, she would enter a different life, without the hope of love. She stood over his limp body. Her sobs quieted. Her curses became whispers, then stopped, replaced by subdued snarls like snarls of an animal crouching, about to strike. The deepest feelings of her life swirled together in a cataract of overwhelming emotion that buffeted her and sucked her down.

Run away or stay? Weep for lost love or strike back? She cried out like a wounded animal and began to dart about the room as the two sides of herself battled for ascendancy. Then suddenly she felt an almost physical jerk, as if a bond had been broken. She rushed around the room in a frenzied circle. On the second circle, she paused at the table against the wall, where he had laid out his treasures--the amphora of wine, a couple of embroidered napkins, a crystal glass or two--and the jeweled dagger, all apparently gifts from women. With a snarl, she snatched up the dagger. For a moment she caressed it, stroked it, held it to her bosom and warmed it. She felt as if something within her that had been imprisoned was suddenly free.

Clutching the dagger, its gemstones warm in her hand, she crept back to the bed, where he lay gently snoring. He lay on his stomach. His back, glowing in the candlelight, was a rejection of her and their love, a closed door. She hovered over him for a moment. Then with a cry she thrust the dagger down, down into his back, crunching against bone. Blood gushed, warm and wet through her tunic. And her flesh recoiled from its warmth and wetness. She pulled the dagger back and thrust again and yet again. He groaned once and threw up his arms; his head jerked back, and even in the dark she saw his face twist and saw the surprise and the question in his eyes. She thrust again, and then he was still.

She cried out and spread her arms like a bird of prey about to take off with its kill. Then suddenly her rage, slaked, left her, whipped away like petals in a strong wind, and she came to herself sobbing and moaning, bending over the beloved body, butchered and bloody like raw meat, his eyes staring in dull surprise, his mouth open. The dagger slipped from her hand and clattered on the stone floor. Blood was everywhere. His arm flopped over the side of the bed, the fingertips lightly brushing the floor. In the shadows, he seemed to move, alive even in death. The fleecy white blanket was dappled with scarlet.

And now the last candle flickered out, and darkness silently engulfed the room. She couldn't tell whether her eyes were open or closed. She dashed in panic from the room, out into the streets. Ran, frantic. Ran from the inconceivable thing. Ran through the dark streets, her tunic cold from the wet blood; she ran unseen and unheeded, invisible. Ran--to where? Where was there to run? Ran home to the only warmth she had ever known. Ran home, bloody and crazy, to Marcella.

Here on the mountain, the memory washing over her in a wave of horror, she no longer felt the shuddering earth.

THE DAY THE GODS WEPT

VIII

The dog Dora cowered under Longinius' bed, shuddering and silent except for an occasional whimper. She had raced around the room frantically, running into the bed, the chair, and the wall in her near-blindness and her great fear. Finally Longinius had come and tied a long rope around her neck and tethered her to the bed. "What's wrong, girl?" he had muttered, and even if she had had the gift of speech, she could not have told him. She fought the rope after he left the room, and it jerked her neck until she was almost senseless, but finally she gave up and now cringed beneath the bed, shaking and silent. Waiting.

***

It was nearly noon. The sun was relentless. Sweat clung to Lucius' body, clammy and unclean. It had been a shitty morning. Lucius' world was somehow off-kilter, not quite predictable, like an oven that, without your knowing it, was too hot or not hot enough, and the dough that you put into it turned out dried-up and hard on the outside or pallid and raw on the inside. But they had managed to get through the morning with the women doing the baking and Lucius waiting on the customers. The morning rush was over now, and usually Lucius would be going to relax in a soothing bath and then have lunch in the tavern.

But today he would have to head down toward the theater district to find that boy Fabius and ask him whether he had seen Valeria-Julia. He would wrestle later with the irksome changes which seemed to be coming about in the bakery. He thought about Augusta and how good it would be to get home to her later on and relax in the glow of her love. He thought about the new life budding within her, a life which he had planted.

"I'm going out," he announced to Petronia and Statia, as he did every day at this time. He wiped away the prickly sweat which clung to his neck. He started down Stabia Street toward the theater district.

***

Tertius paused and peered up and down the street. Which way did she go?--old Marcella, blind and crippled--where would she go? A quick glance down Vicolo del Panettiere with its shops and bakeries, then the other way toward the Central baths. No. Nowhere. How could she have disappeared so fast? Down toward the Temple of Isis! Yes! He rushed down Stabia street, his eyes raking the crowds.

By now his breath came short as a panting dog's, and his heart pumped furiously, as much from some vague fear as from fatigue. His thoughts whirled like debris in a summer storm. Something was wrong with today. What? What was it? Marcella knew. Marcella was wise. People said that she was crazy, but she knew.

Valeria-Julia. Somewhere in deep trouble. He knew. Marcella could sense it.

Let him find Marcella. Something was wrong with today. Slavery had taught him to heed his instincts. And he knew. Something was wrong with today.

As his thoughts whirled, his eyes darted like sword thrusts. Down Stabia Street, searching the crowds that meandered past large shops, houses, and a dyers' workshop with its furnace and boilers running even in this heat. No glimpse of Marcella. Where was she?

"Tertius! Hey--Tertius!" Someone was calling him.

He stopped suddenly, and a child running behind him collided into his back. The child, giggling, ran on. "Who's that?" Tertius glanced around frantically. A man was trotting toward him from across the street. It was one of Lucius' steady customers.

"You looking for Marcella?" the man called. "--the old woman who used to tell fortunes?--"

"Yes!" Tertius couldn't believe his good luck. "Have you seen her?"

The man, approaching from the other direction, sprinted toward Tertius. "She's right around the corner on Abundance Street, right in front of the barber shop. Man, she's lost her mind! Poor soul, she's yelling and screaming at people to run, get out of Pompeii. Talking about the gods were going to destroy it all. Some folks are laughing at her, some folks just look disgusted. Some of us would help her, poor old thing, but we don't know what to do. She's really gone crazy now! Good thing Lucius sent you--"

But Tertius was off. He dashed down the street and around the corner. A block up, he saw a little knot of people. Two women had left the crowd. One was laughing. "Craziest thing I ever saw. Can you imagine?" The other admonished her. "Well, it's not funny. She's just old. Needs to be locked up somewhere before--" The two women passed by, intent upon their errands.

Marcella was on the stony sidewalk where she had fallen. She was struggling to get up, but nobody was helping her. The people shrank from her, afraid to touch her, afraid that touching her would make them part of what she was. Would give credence to her awful vision. So they shunned her, and some laughed, and some turned away troubled.

"Run, run, you people!" she was shouting in a voice surprisingly strong. "It's now! It's happening now! Get out! Run! Now!" She was on her hands and knees, feeling around desperately for her cane, feeling for something that she could hold onto, something that would help her get back on her feet. "Valeria-Julia! Oh, where is my child?"

The people laughed to think of someone that old having a child. But their laughter was uncomfortable, and they turned away.

Tertius knelt beside the struggling old woman. "Marcella! Marcella!" She grew suddenly still at the unbelievable sound of a familiar voice, the touch of a gentle hand.

"It's me," he said gently, "Tertius. Come let me help you."

"Tertius--Tertius--"

"Where is your stick?"

"I lost it, and I fell. Where are we?"

He lifted her, and they stood together. Marcella trembled on her weak limbs, and she clung to him to keep from falling again. "On Abundance Street," he said in answer to her question, "not far from the temple."

She was shaking with weakness and pain and fear. Tears dropped from her sightless eyes and meandered down her face, pooling in the wrinkles. "Where is Valeria-Julia?"

"I don't know," said Tertius softly, drawing her to him. "Lean on me, we'll go find her."

"It's too late," Marcella whispered. "Even the gods will weep at what they themselves have done."

And she clung to Tertius, an old woman blind and lost, clinging to the young and strong, both of them doomed.

***

Augusta would soon be in her lover's arms. Why did she not feel the excitement today? The glow of budding passion? Instead Lucius kept intruding upon her thoughts--Lucius, almost as old as her father, Lucius, who had changed her life as a farm girl with no future except feeding hogs and digging potatoes, and had given her new life filled with theater and jewelry and new dresses from Napoli. And something else: some sense of who she was and what she might become. She felt out of sorts, not at all in the mood for an amorous encounter. Well, soon her lover would tire of her anyway; men did not particularly like to romance pregnant women. Regardless of how the pregnancy came about. She thought of the gifts she had given him--the soft white blanket, some fruit and cheese and wine, the jeweled dagger. Even, occasionally, a round of bread from the bakery. She wondered suddenly why she had given him the dagger. It had been a gift which Estella had given Lucius to celebrate some milestone of their success. A strange gift! In her ongoing effort to erase Estella's presence in what was now her house and in a particularly angry pique with Lucius, she had filched the dagger and given it to her lover. She smiled bitterly to herself. Was it less painful to be stabbed with a jeweled dagger than with a plain one?

Augusta was not given to thought and analysis. Like the rest of us, she had no way of knowing that insight into the self is the first step toward change and she herself was on the brink of change. She was too young to realize that people can change, even on the most profound level. She was too young to appreciate the empowerment of that realization. So she trudged, puzzled by her own reluctance, toward the tryst with her lover, not heeding her subliminal concern that the August sun scorched like living fire, and no birds sang.

And if the earth moved beneath her feet, perhaps it was her life that was changing, shifting, becoming different.

***

Lucius strode down Stabia Street, prodded by a troublesome uneasiness which was becoming sharper and more focused by the second. He was certain now that something terrible had happened to Valeria-Julia, and his mind ran through a catalog of awful possibilities. And what were they to do about Marcella? Old people could be such a problem. He cringed at the memory of the unpleasant scene with Marcella that morning. And Tertius--slaves were not supposed to just run off like that. Lucius was not good at punishing servants and slaves. Damn! And his thoughts snapped back to his worry about Valeria-Julia. Anxiety and fury gave strength to his tiring legs. And resentment. Here he was, caught up in a mess that he didn't create, his schedule disrupted, here he was, hot and hungry, weary, angry-- And worried. Where was Valeria-Julia? Was she safe? Was she hurt? That boy might know--the actor--Fabius--Lucius had seen them talking together, whispering and smiling and touching. He had never seen her so radiant. She had seemed to be almost another person. Maybe she was with Fabius. But surely she should be back by now. Had Fabius done something to her? Had he hurt her in some way?

Damn! What a day! What a mess! He flicked the sweat out of his eyes and wiped his forehead with his sleeve. His eyes searched the streets for Valeria-Julia somewhere among the people who went about their daily activities, Valeria-Julia going back toward the bakery, late but intact. Oh! There she was!--heading up the other way! He called to her and rushed across the street--but as he got closer, shouting the name, the girl looked through him and beyond him, continuing on her way, and he saw that she was not Valeria-Julia. Embarrassed, he plodded on.

Damn! His world was eroding beneath his feet. Under his worry and irritation, beyond his physical discomfort, was a longing for the evening when he would be with Augusta, sipping wine poured from the amphora of Vesuvinum, when he would hold her softness and deeply, slowly inhale her lemony scent and be intoxicated not by wine but by desire.

His thoughts must have created a disturbing reality, for ahead of him, about to turn into the court behind the small theatre, he thought he saw Augusta. He increased his pace, got closer. That was Augusta!

"Augusta!" he cried, but the woman was too far away and she did not hear. And beneath his feet, the earth trembled.

***

Lost on the familiar mountain, without landmarks or paths, Valeria-Julia began to weep, softly at first but then building into heavy sobs. The skin on her face and arms stung. Her damp garments clung and her feet were swollen and raw. Her ankle hurt and was swelling horribly. She stumbled from rock to bush to tree seeking shelter, but there was no shelter. Finally, exhausted, she dropped down under a tree, but even there the sun, directly overhead, ferreted her out. Her sobs quieted. Crouching beneath the tree, she pressed her wet forehead against her knees and closed her eyes.

The world was intensely silent. No breeze rustled the leaves. No birds sang.

In a terrible epiphany, Valeria-Julia realized the horror of her plight. She had killed Fabius! Her jumbled mind replayed that moment with agonized clarity. Over and over, she felt the thrust of the dagger through flesh, the gush of hot blood. Fabius!

She wanted to go home. She would find her way home. To Marcella. Marcella had loved her when no one else had. When she hadn't loved herself. She would find her way home to Marcella.

***

Augusta thought she heard someone calling her name, "Augusta!" But a wicked breeze had started and was thrusting sounds behind her. "Augusta!!" Perhaps it wasn't a voice at all--probably not--but only a distorted wailing of the wind. She leaned forward into the rising wind, her soft muslin dress fluttering behind her. Dammit! Her hair would be ruined. She felt a strange apprehension. There was something unnatural about this sudden vicious wind. She was hurrying now, partly toward the illusory security of her lover's arms but mostly toward the shelter of a strong and impenetrable building.

"Augusta!" Her father's voice? Her husband's? Or a distorted sound of the mounting wind?

At last---she shoved open the heavy door of the building and ducked into the dark hallway. At last she was sheltered from the probing wind. The door of her lover's room was ajar. Good--he was waiting for her.

"Augusta!"--the wind, surely the wind outside.

She flung open his door. But even as she stepped forward into the room, his name on her lips, she recoiled backward in horror. For her lover lay naked on their bed of joy, his face turned toward her, his eyes wide and still, his blood everywhere. Like a slaughtered hog.

.

"FA-BI-US!!" she screamed, loud and long, clinging to each syllable.

Vaguely she heard the outer door open. "Augusta!" bursting into the room behind her.

***

On the mountainside, Valeria-Julia crouched in the weeds and waited. The world seemed outside of her essential self. There was no reality for her except the storm within. She was somewhere between exhaustion and madness. The mountain was before her, the city far behind. She had lost the road between. She was torn between the chaos within and the unnatural silence of the mountainside. She crouched immobilized. Terrible images flashed through her, and guilt and triumph warred. Fabius was dead. Fabius was dead, and she had killed him, and love had died with him, and hope had died with him, her beautiful Fabius with the sun in his hair.

IX

B-O-O-M!!

A roar of thunder shattered the world. Roar after roar of thunder, deafening, shattering. Earth reeled. Instinctively the people turned toward the mountain, all eyes riveted on the unthinkable, the impossible thing. Their lives dropped away. The previous instant, as well as all the years before, became the irretrievable past. With the first clap of thunder, they were lost in uncharted chaos.

The top of Vesuvius had blown off. The people stared unbelieving. A plume of white and gray and black shot upward from the summit, miles into the air, like the trunk of some gigantic tree. For the top of the mountain had blown off. A hideous cloud shot from it, its evil gray trunk spreading into wide branches at the top like an umbrella pine tree, its branches expanding like inexorable fate. As the people stared, transfixed, the top reached out, and then night dropped upon them at midday and winter winds whirled around them in midsummer, and sharp pellets hurled about them, piercing their flesh. They ran for shelter, not knowing in their panic and in the opaque darkness that there was no place to hide.

Lost and half-crazed on the mountainside, Valeria-Julia was jerked into a different reality. The earth, the only stability she had known, rocked beneath her, and she fell to the ground. The silent mountain roared like an enraged beast. From where she had fallen, she clutched the trembling grass. All the fear and hurt of her life rained down upon her in pellets and stones and a fiery, indefinable mass. On her knees she scrambled over the rocking ground and squatted beneath a sturdy bush. But there was no shelter there. No shelter anywhere. The immovable mountain lurched beneath her, and though she clung to a tree trunk, the tree was rocking, too, and nothing, nothing was stable and there was no life that she could go back to, for she had killed her Fabius, killed her dream and strangled in its blood.

***

The dog Dora's neck was raw and bloody from her struggles against the leather collar which bound her to her doom. Screaming wildly, she jerked against the collar, her body twisting into peculiar shapes, her old dugs flopping. But nobody came to release her, and nobody heard above the din outside, and nobody remembered the old bitch in the house guardian's room, battling for life.

***

Marcella and Tertius had reached the Temple of Isis. She leaned on him heavily, for without her cane, the fragile hips and knees could not support her weight. When the explosion came, she jerked her head toward the mountain and opened her eyes wide. She could not see the awful cloud, but she knew. She knew. The prophesy. Oh, if only she could have been wrong !!

The wind was whipping her garment around her thin body, and she clung to Tertius, whose sturdy arm kept her from falling. She thought briefly of her own lost son and what it would have been like to have him here, helping her in her helplessness. But the wind shrieked like a puma about to strike. And even in her darkness, she knew that the sighted, like her, must now grope their way through the dark. She would have to let him go. Perhaps he would be one who would escape.

"It's so cold," she muttered, for a brief moment pressing closer to him.

She wanted to live. Even with all her accumulated years, hard years, even with her blindness and her loneliness and her pain, even with her sense that nobody had ever known her and thus loved her, something in her wanted to live. Like all of us, she feared the unknown adventure of death.

She was trembling violently now and could hardly stumble along. Tertius was practically dragging her. "Too late--," she gasped. "Can't find her now. Too late. You go on. Too late now--"

"We're here at the temple." His voice was rigidly controlled, but Marcella could sense his panic.

"Leave me here on the steps. That's where it began for me."

"No, let me take you inside where you'll be safe."

"Safe from the gods?" She eased herself onto the steps where the vision had come to her so long ago. "Run out of here, Tertius. Hurry! There may be time for you."

"Valeria-Julia..."

"It's too late now. You can't find her. Go east, Tertius, to the Sarno, down to the sea. There will be people in boats. Maybe you can find space. Run, go now!" He started to protest, but she interrupted desperately. "I can crawl up the steps into the temple if I have to, or someone will help me. You go! Go now-- Live!"

And in that moment of his hesitation to leave her in the extremity of approaching death, Marcella felt the power of being loved. "Go on," she said, gently now.

He surrendered to his desire to live. He fled.

Marcella huddled on the edge of a step, out of the way of the people who were beginning to scurry in and out of the temple. She folded into herself as much as her stiff limbs would permit. She turned her back to the wind and endured the pebbles that pelted her. Instinctively she ducked her head into her shoulders and clasped her gnarled hands over her head as if they could protect it. She saw images of her long life, and her final thoughts were of Valeria-Julia, her gift from the gods. Did the child ever love her? Even now she could not know. But the gift was not the receiving of love but the opportunity to give love. And for some of us, that is enough.

Marcella crouched on the steps of the temple. Perhaps in her senility she was unaware of what was happening, or perhaps in her wisdom, culled from all those years of living, she had learned acceptance.

She heard neither the rising wail of the wind nor the cries of the people who only moments ago had jeered at her revelation of truth.

***

"Augusta!" At the instant of Lucius' cry, the explosion swallowed all other sound, and Lucius' puny scream was lost. His open mouth and his flailing arms were invisible in the sudden dark. But he screamed again, unheard and unseen. In his incomprehensible panic, he had no other language and no other word to cry out except her name.

He knew that she could neither see nor hear him now, and he knew that he was plunged in confusion and could not find a way. He groped through the open door, groped along the wall because he had no other direction, and because beneath the rumble of thunder and the wail of the wind, he heard nearby the sound of whimpering and gasping for breath.

"Augusta!" Beneath the stench of blood and shit and fear, he detected close by him the delicate scent of lemon. "Augusta!"

His fingers felt the soft flow of fabric and under that, the softness of flesh and the cold damp of sweat. She came to him, clasped him, and moaned his name, or what might have been his name: Neither could hear nor see the other. Her cold hand clutched his wrist like the clutch of a vulture's claw. He half-led, half-dragged her down the steps to the heavy front door of the building. They crouched there, clinging together, and waited for the storm to pass.

***

Tertius fled back to Abundance Street, picking his way in the dark through the rising debris, pursued by the conflict between guilt and self-preservation. He should have stayed with Marcella; he should have looked for Valeria-Julia; but what good could he have done? For life as they knew it had ended. But his visceral feelings insisted that he needed to save himself. Whatever life was, however it could be defined, he had to fight to preserve it. So he fled. Down to the gate at the Sarno River. Away from Pompeii. Away anywhere. To the sea. To find a boat. Water would save him. To the sea, where water was the way from death to life.

Darkness at midsummer noon. Sheets of flame pouring from the sky. Hot winds blasting through his thin summer garments. He rushed on, frantic. Stones and even rocks hurtling from the black sky. The ground heaved, and he fell. He struggled to his feet bruised and bleeding and he fell again. He groped through a thick and sulfurous darkness. His breath came short and rapid, but breathing was tortured: burning ash, falling from the sky, and smoke and an evil stench seared his lungs. Wind-blown debris stung his eyes. He shielded them with shaking hands, but even with his eyes wide open, he could see little. Violent lightning flashes cutting through the darkness and sheets of fire from the sky revealed horrifying glimpses of crowds pushing and shoving and scurrying. Some were holding planks and broken tiles over their heads. Everybody rushed intently in diverse directions, as if each knew where to find shelter. People jostled each other, and some fell, some were crying out and others ran in stony-faced silence; some carried children or dragged them by the arm, some ran in groups helping each other along, and some ran alone. There were elderly people who limped along alone and some who leaned on younger people, slowing them down in their mad flight to nowhere.

In the dark Tertius could sense only shadowy figures who shoved him or fell against him or whom he stumbled over in his rush to the sea. Beneath the roar of the thunder and the crash of the rocks was a rising chorus of moans, screams, and prayers: Some prayed for delivery, and others prayed for death. Some cursed the gods. Others simply huddled silently in doorways. The punishing wind was foul now with a smell like rotten eggs and fear, and stones and rocks pelted them and stunned them and crushed their vulnerable flesh. Buildings rattled and some crashed where the walls were weakened by the reeling earth, crushing those who had sought shelter.

His altered world appeared to him as frozen instants of brilliant light followed by darkness, complete and impenetrable.

Flash!--a woman by his side, her hands lifted to the unseeing gods.

Flash!--a family holding on to each other, the man carrying a child and pulling his wife along, their mouths open in an unheard cry.

Flash!-- someone crawling, one hand stretched in supplication.

Flash!--a crowd pushing on, trampling each other.

Nothing was quite real. Surely this was a nightmare, unbelievable and unreal, from which he struggled to awaken.

***

Crouched inside the doorway of the actors' house, Augusta and Lucius clung together. Neither was concerned with what had brought them to this place at this time; the explosion had obliterated the past and thrust them into a terrible present and an inconceivable future. Through the shut door they could hear the unspeakable scene outside. She was pinned against the wall as he shielded her. She clutched his body, large and sheltering over her, and on some profound level of herself, she knew that in this awful moment, she had found her way home. Lucius was her home. This moment, which was the end of all they had known, even the end of their lives, this moment was also a beginning. They held each other tightly, locked in a fatal embrace.

***

Tertius' forehead and shoulders were stinging and wet with sweat and perhaps blood. A cart ran into his heel and the back of his leg, throwing him to the ground. The man pushing the cart snarled as if the collision were Tertius' fault, pulled back the cart, and rushed on. In a flash of lightning Tertius saw a cart loaded with all sorts of things, spilling out as the man pushed on. A weeping woman stumbled after the man, clutching a strangely limp and silent baby.

Exhausted now, Tertius struggled to his feet, his knees scraped and bleeding and his hands stinging from the fall on the stones, and stumbled on in what he perceived to be the direction to the sea. He was no longer sure of any direction. He couldn't see any of the familiar landmarks, and even the street was rapidly being obliterated by the debris falling from the black sky. There were no longer any boundaries, and he, too, was lost. Running, stumbling, fleeing, lost.

***

On the mountainside Valeria-Julia pressed her back against the trunk of a stout pine. But the earth beneath her shuddered and buckled, and the lowest branches of the tree whipped wildly, beating her about the head and face. In the darkness, sheets of flame flowed down the mountain. But nothing seemed real to her. She had entered a world of dreams. She ducked her head to avoid the pine branches, then peered out and stared unbelieving. Burning lava was hurtling down the mountain, hurtling toward her. And there was nowhere to run.

Valeria-Julia drew her knees to her chin. She clasped her hands over her mouth. And her visceral scream was drowned in the scream of the demented gods.

***

The sea. The waterway. The city's lifeline. If he could only make it to the sea. Marcella had told him to get to the water. A boat. Surely he could find a boat somewhere at the seashore.

Bleeding and limping and dragging one foot, Tertius burst through the gateway and came out at the seashore. But where was the water? He cried one hoarse "NO!!" and then a scream beyond words. His legs collapsed and he sank to the unsteady earth. For the flickering light from the flames and the lightning flashes revealed that the sea had recoiled from them, and dying sea creatures, weird fragments of life that nobody had ever seen before, flopped in the damp sand. In the sick yellow light, pelted by stones and burning ash, having come so far and suffered so much, Tertius flung his fists about in a futile gesture to the gods. Then the wave, hovering high for a frozen instant, struck.

***

The gods screamed with mirth. Power! Oh, they reveled in the power! Once again they had tested their power, they had pushed it to the utmost. And those puny human beings, mere insects, were scurrying frantically to nowhere. And the gods screamed with mirth. For they were the gods! Look what they could do!

After the umbrella cloud had come the dark, a hail of stones and rocks and light pumice pelting the people immersed in darkness except for the awful revelations of the lightning and the flames. The earth had erupted, buildings had rattled and collapsed, all that they had built and created for all the years, were destroyed in an instant, and people had fled or hidden, and each choice was as futile as the last. Some people, before fleeing, had run to their homes to gather their possessions and, laden by their affluence, had struggled on the road to nowhere. Some, clutching their jewelry and money, were crushed in their homes by collapsing roofs. By midnight, parts of the city were waist-high, head-high in debris.

An hour later the eruption ceased, and some of the people picked their way through the rubble trying to return home, because home was their place of safety, certain that the trouble was over except for the rebuilding. They were, they felt, the lucky ones. They had survived.

Lucius and Augusta were crouching on the floor inside the heavy door of the building. He pressed his body between her and destruction, and she clung to him, whimpering. But in the core of her being, below the terror of the destruction and the horror of her discovery of Fabius, was a sense of wonder: In all her life, nobody had ever sheltered her. She flinched whenever flying debris struck his back. His cries and curses and prayers to the gods, even the smell of his fear were strangely comforting. She crouched tightly, protecting the child inside her. The child, who until this time had been, to her, an inconvenience rather than a child. As the world ended, Lucius was her only bulwark. Lucius.

"It's over," he muttered, his voice raspy and hoarse. "Whatever it was, it's all over." Painfully, feeling his age now, he unwound from his cramped position, got to his knees, and holding on to the cracked and crumbling wall, managed to stand. He grasped her by the arm to help her up.

"Lucius--oh, Lucius--"

Holding on to each other, they picked their way through the wreckage of their lives. They hardly knew where they were. The boundaries were gone. A heavy darkness engulfed them, and they had to work their way through rubble. Somewhere she found a plank, which they used to help shove the debris aside, but the way was torturous. Their hands and legs were bleeding. The thin soles of their shoes were torn, and their feet were cut. A stench of blood stifled their breath, made them gasp, made them dizzy. Their minds were stunned. They were lost.

Even as the people picked their way through the nightmare world, a river of burning lava rushed from the heart of the mountain and caught them and flowed over them and the burning lava froze them at the moment of their deaths so that two thousand years hence, the world would see them at this, their most intimate moment.

By now, whatever had been alive in the city was dead. The gardens, the grass, and the healing herbs had all been smothered. The animals and the people, all things that breathed, had been choked by the poison gas.

The gigantic crater collapsed, crushing what was left of the city with Vesuvius' vomit as high as whatever rooftops were left. For days, pumice fell. The city was buried beneath a layer of mud and detritus hilltop high, twice as high at the seashore, a layer solidified rock-hard, preserving Pompeii for posterity.

The city was silent.

And the gods no longer laughed. Seeing what their power had wrought, seeing what they had done simply because they could do it, the gods wept.

Years passed. A lifetime passed. At first the curious came to stare; looters came to search through the rubble, survivors of the eruption, settled now in neighboring towns, returned compulsively to stand on a hill of hardened lava and stare down at the blackened ground that buried the wreckage of their past. A new City of the Dead. A city haunted by life suddenly and violently severed. A haunted city. But as the years passed, curiosity was faded, loot was exhausted, and survivors died out. The ancient city settled into silence as profound as death. The weary ghosts faded into eternity. People began to forget the name Pompeii; eventually it would be called simply "the city," and only the very old would remember that beneath the hill a city had actually lived.

Decades after the eruption, an old man leaning on a staff tottered up the hill. He was pale with the pallor of age and illness and impending death. He trembled from the heat and from weariness, but his eyes glittered with determination, and one side of his mouth curled upward in a sardonic grin--or so it seemed until one saw the scar on the side of his face pulling his lips upward. A younger man in his thirties was holding the old man by the arm and around the waist, supporting him and nearly dragging him up the hill. The two looked as alike as two beans except for the fact that they were a generation apart and the younger man was tanned and fit.

"I still don't see why you had to come," he was complaining. "All these years, you haven't come back here. Why now? You ought to be home in bed."

The old man simply smiled and clung to his son, breathing heavily and rapidly.

In spite of his complaining words, the son's touch was gentle and strong. There was no need and indeed no way for the elderly man to explain his mission.

After much stumbling and stopping to rest, they reached the top of the hill. Both were exhausted; the old man had to stretch out on the hard ground while his son sat on a large rock, his elbows on his knees, his sweaty face in his hands. Gradually their harsh breathing quieted and slowed. The old man wiped his face with a soft cloth. With the help of his son, he struggled to his feet and, leaning heavily on his staff, gazed hungrily at the barren scene before him and around him, gazed at the bright sky and the ground hard and still black beneath his swollen feet, turned this way and that way, his eyes bright with emotion. The son stood nearby, silent but vigilant.

The father whispered, more to himself than to his son, "I was a slave here."

"I know."

"I wish I had kept the belt I had to wear that showed that I belonged to another man. I wish I had kept it. I cut it off that terrible day, with a piece of broken glass. I've told you about that. I flung it into the inferno. I felt--I wish I could tell you how I felt, to throw that belt away!"

"Yes. But why would you wish you had kept it? It was a sign of slavery!"

The old man pounded his staff upon the earth impatiently, not so much with impatience for his son's lack of understanding but rather for his inability to explain. "Yes," he said finally, "but it meant freedom, too. Because I got it off. I got it off and I found my freedom!."

"Yes," was all that the son said.

"Do you know what is buried beneath this ground?"

"Yes, sure. You've told us all about that."

The father smiled a little and shook his head gently, then whispered again, "Do you know what is buried beneath this ground?"

The younger man soon began to grow restless and increasingly concerned about his father, whose surge of strength seemed to be waning. "I guess we'd better be starting back. We've still got a ways to travel, and Mother will start to worry. And I've got an awful lot to do getting the new crop in. Are you ready to go?"

At first the old man seemed not to hear. Then he turned to his son as if he were returning from far away. "Yes--of course. I'm ready. I can go home now."

As they started the precipitous downward journey, the old man stopped. He looked up to his son, on whose arm he leaned for support and balance. "Thank you," he said simply. The younger man had no reply, being rather bumbling at expressing feelings, but his arm tightened around his father's waist in something of an embrace.

They started down the hill again. After a few steps, the father stopped once more. He pointed with his staff to the surrounding landscape. "Look, can you believe it? Grass has grown on this hill. Some little trees and shrubs have started to grow, just a few here and there. And oh look! Listen to that! The birds have come back!"

And they started again down the hill, heading for home.

Time passed and time stopped. The fiery lava froze the city's agony and the splendor of its past. In its wake homes and shops, hovels and villas, statues and fountains, temples and seats of government had crumpled and splattered in streets and courtyards. The people slept in the postures in which death caught them. A young woman, crouched beneath a fallen tree on the mountainside, looked unbelievingly at approaching death and covered an eternal scream with frantic hands. Beside the ruined steps of a temple a thin adolescent girl curled around a baby she was trying to protect; a basket containing two loaves of bread had dropped on the ground at her feet. In the ruins of a house a little dog sprawled on her back, legs akimbo, body twisted, chained to a bed. Two thousand people in bizarre attitudes of death. Waiting. Waiting as the centuries slipped past.

On the outside, the deadly hill yielded to time. Rain and sun and wind wrought a gradual miracle. Ashes and cinders softened, blackened earth transformed to rich dark soil. A living city grew over the dead.

On top of all that death, grass grew again.

Made in the USA
Middletown, DE
17 October 2022